Hard Knocks High

Project Windows

KEVIN BROWN

Hard Knocks High: Project Windows

Jank Publishing

ISBN-13: 978-0-9845572-0-2
ISBN-10: 0-9845572-0-2

Library of Congress Control Number: 2014914480

www.hardknockshigh.com

Dedicated to my girls.
My inspiration, my motivation and my reason.

Chapter 1

A drum roll of gunshots exploded on the other side of Tafari King's bedroom window. Within seconds, or so it seemed, a symphony of police-siren sopranos wailed like off-key background crooners. Tafari scrambled toward the noise and clumsily fell into a seat on the cold radiator. He pressed his face against the stained window glass, eyes darting back and forth, sweeping the streets for the lifeless body of a young thug sprawled out on the cold pavement, leaking his life liquids into the open wounds of the cracked sidewalk, but to no avail. His eyes searched for another young thug, upright, legs pumping away from a gruesome scene with a gun handle in his fist, but still no dice.

Just down the block, in the area where he could have sworn the gunshots erupted, the sound of a basketball thumped a steady tempo as if the basketball court was an African bass drum. And just like an African calling, Tafari watched from his sixth floor window as boys, some with basketballs tucked under their arms, emerged from all corners of the projects and bopped toward the asphalt drum. To the left of his window, a group of boys wearing baseball caps tilted to the side, leaned against parked cars and nodded in unison to the bass that thumped from one of the parked jeeps. Laughter erupted from the flock as a few girls with hands raised high over their heads danced in the middle.

More background noise was provided by the chit-chat of gray-bearded men with distant stares as they shuffled in and out of the liquor store. Other men, some balding, others not so much, were all slumped over on crates as if the weight of the project buildings behind them were actually perched on top of their shoulders while they played dominoes. They fussed, argued, and chanted as the competition heated up. Before long, the faint echo of the gunshots and the wailing sirens blended superbly with the bass, the laughter, the fussing, the honking horns of cars, the thumping basketball, and the rest of the incoherent background noise that formed the projects' music.

Tafari's eyes drifted across the street to the main noise makers outside of his window: Lil' Headache, Stretch, and Los. Although Tafari didn't know them personally, just by listening to their conversations from his window seat and seeing them in the halls of Bronx High, he knew

Lil' Headache's real name was Damian, Stretch's real name was Alphonso, and Los was short for Carlos. They were the lead thug characters he watched perform on the corner every night from his radiator seat. That evening, they were across the street, huddled together in front of the deli, like pigeons in the winter. They two-stepped under a cloud of weed smoke as a beat with heavy bass thumped from a double-parked black Escalade. The gunshots weren't enough to interrupt their dance, since none of them missed a step when the shots rang out. In fact, *nobody* on the other side of his window missed a beat. It was as if Tafari was the only one who heard the gunshots.

After several more minutes of carefully observing the boys on the corner, Tafari rose from the radiator, no longer looking *through* the glass, but looking *at* it and staring back at him was a face that looked like his. His twin with the cinnamon skin sported a low haircut and long sideburns. The face in the glass scowled at Tafari similar to the way Lil' Headache and his boys scowled at foreigners who dared to wander past their corner. The boy in the glass pointed in Tafari's face and in a voice that sounded like his, grunted, "Whatchu lookin' at?! Huh?! Yeah, I'm talkin' to you! Whatchu gonna do?! Huh?!" Tafari never flinched at any of the threatening words or the mad faces he tried on because he knew *him* too well. It was Tafari's inner thug. The same inner thug that hid behind his eyes only to reveal himself when Tafari was alone, standing in front of a mirror or anything with a reflection. An inner thug he hid and never revealed to anyone.

Tafari put on a pair of oversized headphones and nodded his round head to the rap song while his body swayed back and forth dancing the same two-step Lil' Headache performed on the corner. Suddenly, there was a loud rap on his bedroom door. He snatched the headphones from his ears and tossed the portable CD Player onto his twin bed and buried it beneath his pillow.

"Yeah!?" Tafari called.

"It's Leon and Noel," two voices harmonized. Tafari opened the door and was greeted by his twin neighbors, both wearing identical black suits with gray ties. The twins click-clacked across the wooden tiles, following Tafari into his room before jumping on the bed and sandwiching Tafari in the middle.

"Whatcha listening to?" Leon asked, as Tafari pulled his CD Player from under the pillow.

"A CD."

"Why are you listening to that old CD Player? Don't you have an iPod?"

"Yeah. I got an iPod. But my mom is always checking it to make sure I don't have any inappropriate music on it." Tafari held up the CD Player. "That's what this is for. She don't know nothin' about this."

"That's a good idea," Noel declared. "Mom be downloading these lame Disney-rap songs onto me and Leon's iPod. We are thirteen years old. We don't wanna hear no kiddy rap. We need to get us a CD Player that Mom don't know nothin' about, too."

"Fareal," Leon agreed.

"Mom be trippin'," Noel continued. "She don't let us have any fun."

"Hey, I'm three years older than you guys and I don't get to have any fun either," Tafari cut in, not wanting to be outdone. "I have to go to Bible study every Wednesday, these lame teen rap sessions every Friday, and then church on Sunday."

"Yeah, but at least you're free on Monday, Tuesday, Thursday, and Saturday," Leon pointed out. "We have to go to prayer meetings and youth group meetings. We only have Saturdays off. Tafari, you got it good compared to us."

"Yeah, I guess I do."

"So what do you do on those free days?" Noel asked.

"Those days are free for me to look out of my window at the thugs on the corner all night long. Actually, if it were up to Mom, I wouldn't have a window in my room at all. She don't want me to see the streets, let alone step foot in them. If I'm not going to Bible study or to the teen rap sessions, the only time she lets me go out is to run down to C Town to buy some seasoning salt, vegetable oil, or something that she might need to finish cooking dinner that night."

"Those days are also free for you to listen to rap CDs," Leon mentioned.

"That's right." Tafari nodded. "As long as my door is locked and Mom can't get in."

"So, can we listen to what you're listening to?" Noel asked.

"Yeah, we wanna hear something with some cussin' on it," Leon added, grinning devilishly.

"You know ya mom don't want y'all listening to no gangsta rap."

"Ya mom don't want you listening to it either." *The twin has a point*, Tafari conceded.

"Please," Leon begged. Their eyes were bubbling with curiosity. Tafari looked over at the half-open door and ordered Leon to close and lock it. He leapt from the bed and slid halfway to the door with his scuffed Payless shoes. Leon locked the door and jumped back on the bed beside his brother.

"Y'all better not tell ya mother I let y'all listen to this," Tafari warned.

"We won't." Leon and Noel pressed their faces together like conjoined twins, stretching the headphones wide enough so they could wear them together. As soon as Tafari hit play on the CD player, the twins' eyes and mouths popped open as the shocking, vulgar lyrics poured into their virgin ears for the first time. Within seconds, shock gave way to mischievous excitement. The twins fell back on the bed, rolling around giggling and snickering while they pressed the headphones to their ears. Tafari pressed the stop button when the song ended.

"Hey, why did you stop the music?" Leon asked.

"That's enough for now," Tafari replied.

"Where did you get this CD?" Noel asked.

"From the deli. Papi be selling mixtapes and CDs in the front of the store."

"We wouldn't even know the latest CDs to buy because our mom don't let us listen to any of the hip hop stations on the radio and she rarely lets us watch TV, so we don't get to see any music videos," Leon revealed.

"I know whatchu mean," Tafari added. "My mom doesn't want me to watch BET and MTV. But she can't stop me from looking out of my window."

"What does ya window have to do with music?"

"You can't help but hear music from my window. Jeeps spinning twenty-inch chrome rims are always speeding through the block, tossing bass out of the trunk, vibrating the streets and my window. Then, the jeeps disappear around the corner, dragging the bass and rhymes with them. It's like a tease. I wanted more. I needed more."

"And that's when you went out and bought the CDs?"

"Yeah. As soon as I bought the CDs, I locked myself in my room and nodded to the bangin' beats. But after a while, the beats didn't hold my attention anymore. It was like I lost an ear for it and grew a new one for the lyrics and wordplay. Man, I eat up every word them rappers feed to me through my headphones as if they are vitamins. I'm just amazed with the way some of these rappers can paint vivid pictures and still make it rhyme and make so much sense. It made me wanna give it a try."

"You be writin' rhymes, Tafari?" Leon asked, excitement in his voice.

"Yeah, man," Tafari said, holding up his black and white composition notebook. "I bought a notebook and started writin' my own rhymes. I carry this notebook everywhere I go and I write religiously. In my room before school. In my room after school. In school during school. I just can't put the pen down."

"Kick a rhyme for us," Noel insisted.

"Nah, y'all wouldn't understand."

"Yes we would. Stop frontin' and kick somethin'." Just as Tafari opened his rhyme book, his mother called out from the hall, "Tafari, the phone!"

"I'm coming!" Tafari warned the twins again, "Remember, don't tell anyone I let y'all listen to that CD." They nodded. He placed the Walkman in his backpack next to the Bible and his rhyme book.

It was a little after 5:00 p.m. Almost time for him to leave for Bible study. The click-clacking of his black Buster Browns were muffled once he entered the narrow hallway and stepped on a stream of carpet that stretched down the hall and spilled into an ocean of blue in the living room. Tafari turned left at the end of the hall and into the kitchen.

His mom stood with her back to the window and her arms folded. She was an itty-bitty thing, about five-foot-nothing and barely one hundred pounds soaking wet. The tan housecoat she wore nearly swallowed her whole. Only the tips of her matching tan slippers poked out from the bottom of her housecoat, which hung like dingy stage-curtains, and her small face barely reached out of the flipped up collar. Mom's face was the color of oatmeal and her worn, worrisome eyes were about as dark as dried raisins. Her eyes seemed to get darker with each passing skyline; that is, each passing skyline removed from her being with Tafari's pops.

Tafari never met his dad and didn't know much about him. All he knew was that he bounced when he was a baby and never returned. He never bothered to ask Mom any questions about his dad because he figured the less he knew about him, the less pain he had to deal with.

Speaking of pain, Tafari really hoped it wasn't his annoying cousin, Vaughn Little, on the other end of the phone. Vaughn was the only one that called, except for Mahogany Brown. He hoped, no, rooted for Mahogany to be holding the other end of the phone. For years, Tafari met Mahogany and Vaughn at the train station, twice a week, and they would take the five train to the youth center for Bible study and the teen rap sessions. Then, about a year ago, Mahogany's parents were having some marital problems and left the Christian church to become a Jehovah's Witness, thinking it might save their marriage. They were wrong. As a Jehovah's Witness, Mahogany was no longer allowed to attend the church she grew up in, nor the Bible and teen rap sessions at the youth center.

He picked up the phone while adjusting his tie. "Hello."

"Hi, Tafari. It's Mahogany. I called your cell but it went straight to voice mail." The sound of her squeaky voice sent a bunch of butterflies crashing drunkenly in his stomach. Tafari glanced over at Mom.

"Oh, you want some privacy?" she asked. Tafari nodded. "Mahogany and Tafari sitting in a tree," Mom teased.

Tafari buried the phone in his stomach and whispered, "Stop that, she might hear you."

Mom strolled to the living room, laughing. Ms. Green, who was sitting at the head of the table with a cup of coffee steaming in her face, picked up her mug and joined Mom on the sofa. Tafari put the phone back to his ear. "Hey, Mahogany. My cell got cut off because I ain't pay the bill. Sorry 'bout that. Anyway, I'm leaving now so I'll meet you at the train station in a few minutes. You still comin', right?"

"I was gonna sneak out and go with you to Bible study but I think you should leave without me."

"Why?"

"My aunt passed away last night and I have to help my mom cook because my family is meeting up over here at my apartment." Tafari could feel his hand un-adjusting his tie as he listened. He no longer had the desire to go to Bible study. What was the point if he wasn't going to see Mahogany?

"Dag, I'm sorry to hear that ya aunt passed," Tafari apologized.

"Thank you." Mahogany paused, clearing her throat. "But I really wanted to see . . . um . . . I mean . . . be at Bible study tonight." Tafari's mind told him, no, convinced him, that Mahogany was trying to say she wanted to see *him* that night. And he really wanted to see . . . um . . . be at Bible study that night too. That's how he felt. That's what he wanted to say. Instead, he said, "Well, death is something you can't control. There's nothing you can do about it."

"I *really* don't want to be here because it's gonna be so depressing. I hate feeling like that."

"Yeah, I know whatchu mean. But it's all out of respect for ya aunt and ya moms, so just go ahead and do the family thing." Actually, Tafari didn't want her to do the *family thing*; he wanted her to do the *Bible study thing* so he could sneak peeks at her while she was looking somewhere other than in his direction.

"I know." The telephone went silent for a minute. Mahogany's mother broke the silence in the background when she yelled Mahogany's name. Mahogany sucked her teeth, "Tafari, I gotta go."

"Alright, um, I would say I'll see you tomorrow, but you're probably not coming to school are you?"

"I don't know, Tafari. I really don't know. Things are hectic right now. I don't know what's going on . . ." Her mother yelled her name in the background again.

Mahogany yelled back, but in Tafari's ear, "Coming, Mommy!" Then she said, "I'll speak to you later, Tafari."

"Alright, bye." Tafari waited until the dial tone hummed in his ear before he hung up. Tafari didn't feel the need to go to Bible study anymore. He didn't hurry into his dress pants and fly out of the apartment every Wednesday because he wanted to be the first one to stare all up in Ms. Morehead's pie face. Ms. Morehead was the one that conducted the Bible studies and Tafari couldn't stand that witch. He couldn't put his finger on why; he just didn't like her.

Ten minutes after arriving at the youth center, Tafari was supposed to be reading and taking notes as Ms. Morehead instructed but his pen wouldn't allow it. In his mind, the paper morphed into his block. The blue lines took the shape of project buildings and his pen drove recklessly through the alleyways of the buildings like a stolen car with cherry beams flashing in the rearview mirror. By the time he reached the bottom of the page, his pen left behind poetic street tales of him bustin' guns at thugs and running from the cops.

His eyes gazed, satisfyingly, over the lyrical masterpiece that he put together in a matter of minutes. While reciting the rhymes in his head, he felt someone's presence hovering over his shoulder. It was Vaughn. Tafari closed the book in his face. Vaughn smirked and called out, "Ms. Morehead! Ms. Morehead! Tafari's not doing his assignment!"

"Yes, I am!" Tafari snapped.

"No, he's not. He's writing raps. Look in his book." Tafari glared menacingly at Vaughn. Ms. Morehead's eyes rolled back and forth between Tafari and Vaughn like a wheel. It finally stopped on Tafari. He was the lucky winner to feel her wrath.

"Are you done with your assignment, Tafari?"

"No."

"Let me see what you have thus far."

"Um, I didn't start yet, Ms. Morehead."

"Didn't start? Just a few minutes ago I saw you writing up a storm. What were you writing?" Snickering and laughter erupted from every corner of the semicircle of chairs. Even Mahogany was smirking at Tafari. Mahogany? *What was she doing there?* Tafari thought. *She was supposed to be at home grieving with family. When did she walk in?*

There was no way Tafari could let Ms. Morehead see his rhyme book. The curse words, let alone the content, would make poor old Ms. Morehead tumble to the floor from heart failure. Before she flatlined, the witch would hold just enough breath in her lungs to pick up a phone and tell his mother about *his* rhyme book.

Tafari said the first thing that came to mind: "I was just writing in my private journal."

"Was that the assignment I gave? To write in your private journal?"

"No, Ms. Morehead."

"You know what? I think I'm going to call your mother. You've been disconnected the past few weeks." Vaughn snickered behind Tafari. Tafari had visions of grabbing two hands full of his matted-down, sandy afro and slamming him on his back.

Bible study ended at a little before 7:30. Mahogany was the first to rise out of her seat. She stretched a long stretch, threw her arms up, and tangled her fingers together into a ball as if she was dotting an 'i.' Her back arched like the letter 'c,' nearly closed into an 'o' as she continued to bend backwards. She threw her head back and her brown eyes rolled in Tafari's direction before she flashed her straight whites at him. Mahogany snatched her black trench coat from behind the seat and headed for the entrance. Tafari fast-walked and met her there. Actually, he might have skipped. Vaughn rushed over and circled around to the other side of Mahogany as they walked out.

"What are you doing here? Ain'tchu supposed to be home with family?" Tafari asked, excitedly.

"Yeah, but I just slipped out for a minute because I really wanted to see . . . um . . . I mean, come to Bible study." Tafari's smile widened. So did hers. Then he snickered. And she continued to play follow the leader. Vaughn even joined in on the game, smiling and snickering too. But Tafari didn't remember anyone asking him to play. He didn't know about the mind games Mahogany and Tafari were playing. Actually, Tafari wasn't so sure that Mahogany knew that *he knew* about her mind games.

Tafari knew she was there to see him, though. At least that's what the little voice inside was trying to convince him.

"When did you get here?" Tafari asked.

"About ten minutes ago."

"Ya moms don't mind that you left?"

"Actually, I was told to leave. Out of all those pans sitting on the stove and kitchen table, none of them had jerk chicken in them. And that's a first. My aunt's husband's side of the family is Jamaican and I've never been to a family gathering involving my aunt where somebody ain't make jerk chicken."

Tafari still didn't remember anybody asking Vaughn to play, but he invited himself in. "What does jerk chicken have to do with you leaving ya apartment and coming over here?"

"My aunt's husband told me to go to the Jamaican restaurant because he needed some jerk chicken. Since the restaurant is right down the block, I decided to pop into Bible study for a minute."

"But Jackie's Carribean Kitchen is right across the street from you. Why would you take the train for five stops just to come to this one?" Vaughn wondered, still trying to play without knowing the rules.

"Because, I like the jerk chicken over here better." Mahogany couldn't finish that sentence without chuckling. Tafari joined in. Tafari knew that she knew that he knew she didn't ride the train all the way there just to get jerk chicken. They both knew it was a part of the game. But Vaughn didn't know. The puzzled look on his face said so. But he forced out a chuckle anyway. That little red-haired snitch was really starting to annoy Tafari.

They entered the Home Away From Yard Jamaican restaurant at the end of the block and Mahogany placed her order. When Mahogany's food was ready, Tafari and Vaughn fumbled into their pockets and offered to pay. Mahogany waved them off but they insisted. Tafari slapped two crisp five dollar bills on the counter before Vaughn could remove his hand from his pocket. The dreadlocked lady behind the counter gave Tafari two dollars in change and a plastic bag with the food inside.

"Thank you," Mahogany chirped, before throwing her arm around Tafari's shoulder and pressing her cheek on his. Now it was Vaughn's turn to glare at Tafari.

They parted ways once they reached the train station. Parted ways with Vaughn, that is. Vaughn, who usually rode the train home with them, was spending the week at his grandmother's so he was headed to the South Bronx while Tafari and Mahogany were headed back to the northern part of the Bronx. Vaughn extended his arms and tried to hug Mahogany goodbye. Mahogany leaned her shoulder into him without extending her arms and pulled away just as quickly. Tafari was break dancing inside.

Vaughn eyed them from the other side of the platform. His face wrinkled as if he was in pain watching Tafari and Mahogany converse and laugh. Vaughn's train came first. He hurried on and sat by a window, eyeing them until his eyes were swallowed up by the darkness of the tunnel as the train pulled away from the platform.

Tafari and Mahogany's train arrived next. Despite plenty of open seats, they took a seat by the open doors. There was a couple hugged up, whispering and smiling in each other's faces, sitting by the conductor's booth. And there was a heavy-set teen cradling a big bag of cheese doodles sitting across from them. He was bobbing his head like a bobblehead doll to a beat that thumped from his thick headphones.

"I didn't know you kept a journal," Mahogany said as the doors closed.

"Journal? What journal?"

"Didn't you tell Ms. Morehead you were writing in your journal?"

"Oh, nah, I don't have a journal. I just told her that. Actually, I was writin' rhymes."

"Rhymes?"

"Yeah, I be writin' rhymes." Tafari removed the rhyme book from his backpack, opened to the page he wrote the rhymes on during Bible study, and placed it on Mahogany's lap. Her eyes widened as she scanned the page. She read about five seconds before she turned to Tafari with a horrified look in her eyes, "Oh my goodness, Tafari. What's up with all these curses? Why are you talking about shooting people in the face? You don't have a gun!"

"I know. It's just *rhymes*," Tafari laughed.

"If it's just *rhymes*, why does it have to be so violent?"

"That's how everybody raps. I don't mean nothin' by it. I just try to flip ill metaphors and punch lines. Like this rhyme right here." Tafari leaned over and pointed to one of his favorite lines on the page. He rapped out loud,

I'll pull out a pistol

and let a mini-missile

rip through ya skin tissue

then chisel through ya bone gristle

I'll put lead to ya head and give you a holy temple

leave you lying in a hospital bed sippin' your dinner through a straw, lookin' simple.

The dude with the cheese doodles who sat across from them had removed his headphones to give a listen. He nodded at Tafari and said, "Yo, that rhyme was tight, son."

"Good looking out." Tafari reached out and gave him a pound. He drew his hand back and wiped off cheese crumbs on his black dress pant leg. Mahogany glared at Tafari as if he was one of those bums panhandling on the train. "See how I flipped that line? I said, 'I'll give you a holy temple.' You get it? Holy temple like a church. And if I shoot you in your temple, you'll have a hole in it. Get it? Holy temple?" Tafari explained.

"Tafari, that is sick." Mahogany remarked, still glaring at him and shaking her head.

"Whatchu mean sick? Sick like its dope? It's good?"

"Sick like that's disgusting."

"What's disgusting about it?"

"Tafari, you're talking about putting a hole in someone's head. You're talking about pulling out a gun and killing someone. Taking someone's life. Tafari, I'm shocked at you. I didn't know you had this dark side to you."

"Hold up! Hold up! Ya taking this way too serious. I wouldn't really shoot nobody in the head. I told you, it's just rhymes." Tafari tossed his book back into his backpack. "You just don't understand."

"You're right. What I don't understand is why you can't write a nice rhyme about love or something."

"Thugs don't rhyme about love. We rhyme about what's *real* in the streets."

Mahogany threw her hand to her mouth and caught her laughter in her fist. Either she was a little too slow or her fist wasn't tight enough. Chuckles leaked through her fingers and danced in Tafari's ear.

"What's so funny?" Tafari asked.

"You're a thug?" she chuckled.

"Yeah."

"And you know what's *real* in the streets?"

"No doubt."

"How do you know what's *real* in the streets when your mother don't even let you go outside?"

"You just don't get it." Tafari waved her off. He folded his arms and slumped away from her. Mahogany buried her mouth in his shoulder and coughed out more chuckles. She hooked her arm under his. "You mad? I'm sorry, Tafari. I was just joking. You forgive me?" Tafari wasn't really upset, though. And Tafari knew that she knew he wasn't. But it was just a part of the game. A game that Mahogany was playing just as he hoped.

"Yeah, I forgive you." Tafari wanted to seal his forgiveness with a kiss. Wanted to ask her for one but that wasn't part of the game.

"But even the hardest thug has to feel some kind of love, don't you think?" Mahogany asked while lifting her head from his shoulder.

"Yeah, I guess." Tafari shrugged.

"And if you're a good rapper you should be able to write about anything, including love."

"I'm tryna tell you, don't no thug rappers rhyme about love."

"Yes they do. I heard a rap song the other day talking about love. My mother grew up listening to him. What is his name? I think it's, um, L and L too Cool or—"

"You mean LL Cool J. Not L and L too Cool."

"Well, whatever." They laughed together. She continued, "But if he can write about love, you can too. Unless you don't have anyone in particular to write a love song about."

It was like all of sudden, without warning, Mahogany started playing by her own rules. He didn't know what part of the game that was. The unwritten rules in the game they were playing called for its contestants to be safe and cautious. Whenever they came to a fork in the road, they would take the safe, familiar road. The road that would only allow them to circle the block and flirt at a safe distance, kind of like when Tafari would walk to the train station on his way to Bible study. He was too shook to walk by the thugs on the corner, so he would cross the street and circle around. The same way Tafari and Mahogany were circling around the obvious; the *obvious* being their feelings for each other.

Mahogany must have been running out of gas and was growing tired of circling around, so she decided to hit the gas pedal and speed down the unfamiliar road. A waterfall of chills dumped down Tafari's back as feelings he hid from Mahogany for months were slowly being revealed. He shifted and adjusted in his seat when the words crawled to the tip of his tongue. Tafari wanted to tell her. *Wanted* to end the game for good. *Wanted* to tell her about the many dates they had in his mind. *Wanted* to tell her, badly.

Tafari wanted to follow Mahogany's lead but somehow the connection between his mind and tongue got disconnected. The words didn't come out the way he wanted it to. Tafari just couldn't keep from driving cautiously down the familiar road and punked out. "I don't know. I would have to think about that." Mahogany shrunk in her seat. She had the look of a person who was bored of playing the game. Tafari tried to recover by taking a detour and attempted to inch down the road they never traveled.

"But what about you? Do you have someone you like that you might write a rhyme about?" Tafari thought that was a good attempt. But Mahogany was still looking like she didn't want to participate. "I don't write rhymes," she snapped back. The missed opportunity made Tafari slump in his seat. They sat in silence and waited for the other to gather enough confidence to reveal feelings they already knew they had for each other.

Two stops came and went. They had three more stops before they got off the train and headed home. If someone was going to make a move, it had to happen soon, Tafari thought. Mahogany must have had the same thought because she hit the gas and sliced right through the block and into Tafari's gut.

"Are we a couple or what?"

Tafari's car stalled. "Wha-what do you mean?"

"Tafari, we've been together since we were about six years old. Going to Bible study during the week and church at the end—"

"And no outside, no fun, and no nothing in between," Tafari joked.

"True." Mahogany chuckled. "So, we *do* have a lot in common."

"Not everything. I know whats real in the streets."

"Not this again." Mahogany sighed.

"Fareal. Even though I'm not allowed to go outside that much, I practically have a front row seat to the streets. I see drug dealers on the corner, people getting jumped—"

"So do I," Mahogany cut in. "You think I don't have a window in my room too?"

"True. But whatever my window screen doesn't show me, I could always listen to in the poetical street tales on my CD's."

"So, the only thing we don't have in common is you listen to rap CDs. Anything else?"

"Yeah." Tafari swallowed. "You are a lot braver than I am."

"Why do you say that?"

"Remember when we were like twelve and thirteen and you used to let me try out all the new wrestling moves on you?"

"How could I forget? You almost killed me when you put me in the sleeper-hold that one time in my living room."

"Oh yeah. And when you fell, you knocked over the coffee table and broke the picture frame. Thanks for not telling ya mom on me."

"I would never tell on you," Mahogany said, confusion still in her voice. "But why are you bringing this up now?"

"As I got older, I didn't want to bear hug you to make you cry mercy anymore. I wanted to just hug you." Mahogany smiled, glowingly.

"When I was younger, I used to slap the back of your neck during the reverend's long, boring benedictions. But when I got older, I wanted to massage the sting out of the whelps that my love slaps left behind." At that point, Mahogany was glowing so much, she nearly blew a fuse. Tafari continued, "I used to daydream about you in Bible study all the time. Then Ms. Morehead would embarrass me in front of everyone by yelling at me to pay attention and saying she was going to tell my mother. Everyone would laugh. That's why I couldn't stand Ms. Morehead. Always tried to *play me* in front of everyone."

"I never knew that you used to daydream about me."

"And you never would have known if you weren't so brave. I wanted to tell you how much I liked you for a while now, but I was too shy. If you didn't speak up today, I don't think I would have ever told you."

"So, is it official? Are we a couple?" Mahogany asked. A warm sensation blanketed Tafari. The kind of feeling you get after playing a long, tiring game and finally everything sets up perfectly for you. It was the classic double jump to a king. Instead of following Mahogany, when Tafari came to the fork in the road, he went straight.

"Not yet."

"Why not?"

"Real couples kiss," Tafari said, after sneaking a peek at the hugged-up couple by the conductor's booth. Mahogany shivered, as if an electric jolt circulated through her. Her eyes twinkled. Then she smiled.

She rocked back and forth in her seat as if she was cold. Her thin maple brown face was radiant under her ear-to-ear bangs. Mahogany inhaled, seeming to gather herself. Then slowly, her body tipped over toward Tafari. He smelled the Doublemint on her breath as she got closer. Tafari leaned in and their lips met. They stared wide-eyed at each other for a silent count of five. Tafari pulled away first. "Now it's official," Mahogany declared. Her hand crawled into Tafari's and they tangled fingers. They sat still in the moment.

Chapter 2

On a normal Wednesday night, after Tafari and Mahogany's train reached their destination, they would go their separate ways since Mahogany lived on the southside of the projects and Tafari lived on the northside. But there wasn't anything normal about that Wednesday night. That Wednesday night would forever be marked on Mahogany's calendar as the day her and Tafari officially became a couple. And since they were a couple, Tafari felt obligated to walk her to *her* building.

Tafari and Mahogany walked hand in hand through a maze of low and high-rise project buildings, marching like trained soldiers and avoiding any eye contact as boys strolled by in the opposite direction. Thugs uniformed-up in jeans, Timberlands, and oversized baseball caps were guarding the front of each building like security. Each of them had their street faces on to remind anyone that life on that Bronx block wasn't a game.

One of the thugs in front of Mahogany's building stared deep into Tafari's corneas until Tafari's eyes backed down. The thug's presence in the doorway made for a tight squeeze. When Tafari slithered into the lobby, his shoulder nudged the thug's ever so slightly and he silently begged Jesus to give the dude a forgiving heart and let him slide just that one time.

"Thanks for walking me home, Tafari," Mahogany said, excitedly.

"That's what I'm supposed to do. I'm ya boyfriend now, right?" Tafari asked, failing miserably at trying to match her excitement. It was impossible to be anything but nervous when thugs were bopping in and out of the lobby staring at him strangely, as if he had just stepped off of an unidentified flying object. Tafari felt like an open target.

"Yes, you are my boyfriend," Mahogany said with a smile, liking the way it sounded. "Well, I gotta get upstairs, Tafari. I got family to be with and a hungry uncle who's waiting for his jerk chicken."

"Alright. So, I'll see you whenever you are able to come back to school."

"I'll call you in the morning. I'm sure I'll be able to go tomorrow. Maybe we can walk to school together. Would you like that?"

"Yes, I would love to walk you to school." Tafari's words betrayed his very own feelings. He hated the idea of having to walk back to her building in the morning. That is, if he would get away from the building in one piece. Mahogany entered the elevator and waved at Tafari just before the orange door slammed shut, booming in the lobby like a gunshot. The thugs who guarded the door had gathered off to the side to roll dice against the building. Tafari inhaled deeply and held his breath in his cheeks just before he darted through the entrance. Relief blanketed him like a warm hug when he reached the path that led to the northside without a soul in sight.

It was unusually dark out, as if an enormous, sinister, black bird were perched high a top the tallest high-rise building in the projects and blotted out the moon and cast a huge shadow over the projects. Tafari tilted his head and blew the air from his cheeks at the lonely star that sat high atop the black face of night like a Cyclops. Tafari gathered himself and walked, briskly, under the shadowy wings of night.

Without warning, something chilled the back of Tafari's neck and arms. Not the type of chill you get when a light breeze comes sweeping through the block, but the type of chill you feel when some grimy dude comes creeping up on you from behind. The block was unusually hot for an autumn night. It was sauna-like. Because of this, Tafari knew it wasn't a breeze. Quickly, he snapped his neck around to see if anyone was creeping behind him. He didn't see anyone, so he shook it off and continued on the path without a second thought.

Once again, chill bumps grew out of his skin like little warning signals. Tafari stopped in his tracks and his head snapped in the direction of the noise he thought he heard. Again, not a soul was in sight. Just as he turned and started back down the path, out of nowhere, a group of thugs appeared before him as if they had just beamed down from the Star Trek *Enterprise*. Four pairs of low, menacing eyes emerged from the shadows. It was hard to see their faces because they were all hidden by the brims of Yankee hats, pulled down over their eyebrows. There weren't any baseball fields in the projects so Tafari knew they weren't approaching him because they needed an extra player for a friendly game of baseball.

They surrounded him, sealing off any exits. Without any escape routes, Tafari looked off into the distance hoping to see someone, anyone that might be able to help him. Just over Tafari's left shoulder, against a silver gate, were two benches that were occupied by two men sipping out of a bottle wrapped in a brown paper bag when Tafari and Mahogany had walked past ten minutes earlier. But when Tafari looked for the men, the benches were empty.

After years of living in the projects, people kind of develop their own version of spidey-senses. They can feel when something is about to go down. The menacing look on the thugs' faces that had just surrounded him probably had the old men's spidey-senses tingling. And the tingling sensation wasn't from the Smirnoff they were guzzling either. They staggered off into the night before anything went down. They were dying to see what would happen to Tafari, and probably couldn't wait to talk about it the next day, but they ain't want to be nobody's witness.

"Yo, whatchu doin' on my block?" snarled the dude wearing the red Yankee hat.

"I…um…I'm just tryna get home," Tafari stuttered, his heart thundering in his chest.

"What set you claimin', fool?"

"Huh?"

"You heard me. I said what set you claimin'?"

"Oh, nah. I ain't down with no gang."

"Where you live at?"

"I live over there. On the northside."

"Northside? Whatchu doin' over here on my side?"

"I was walking my girl home."

"Ya girl? Nah, that's dead. Ain't no northside dudes allowed to mess with our southside girls. As a matter of fact, northside dudes ain't allowed on the southside at all. You come on our side, you gotta pay rent." Tafari noticed a pair of eyes was missing. There were only three pairs of eyes in front of him, when before, he was sure there were four. The dude in the blue hat patted Tafari's pockets and took the small change he had. "All you got is two dollars?" Blue Hat barked.

"Alright, you got your money. Can I go now?" Tafari pleaded.

"You rushin' us? Huh? You rushin' us!" As Tafari turned to look for the missing eyes, pain exploded on the back of his head. White lightening flashed before his eyes. The pain knifed from the back of his head and stabbed into his forehead. His knees buckled and the concrete seemingly rose up and smashed him on the side of his face. Tafari rolled over on the ground just in time to see a Timberland boot flying toward him with the speed of a javelin. He wanted to react, tried to react, but he was too slow. The tip of the boot stabbed into his ribs. Wind lept out of his lungs and Tafari curled up into a fetal position. Just as he clutched the throbbing pain on the left side of his ribs, more pain exploded from his lower back, his upper back, and left arm. By the time he caught the throbbing pain in one place, more pain erupted somewhere else on his body. The Yankees were beating his butt as if he were wearing pair of red sox.

Seemed like the beat down would never end. The pain was everywhere. After what seemed like forever, the soles of four pairs of Timberlands stopped stomping on him. Tafari moved one of his arms so his left eye could peek out. He saw the Timberlands stomping on the concrete, away from him and down the block.

Tafari didn't know why they stopped, but he was relieved that they did. Slowly, Tafari picked himself off the ground, clutching his aching ribs with one hand and the back of his head with the other. Tafari limped down the path back to the northside with tears pooling in his eyes and scattering down his face.

Tafari was able to make it to his building unseen and slipped into the apartment. He was greeted by Mom's unmistakable cackle from behind her bedroom door. Tafari figured she was watching an old Cosby Show rerun, which is what she would normally watch when he returned from Bible study. With Mom preoccupied by her favorite show, Tafari took two aspirin and gathered a bunch of ice cubes in an old T-shirt. Tafari slipped into a white Hanes shirt and a pair of basketball shorts before easing onto his bed. He cradled the ice pack on his aching ribs. Tears moistened his cheeks and streaked into the corner of his mouth. The tears tasted as bitter as the memories of what happened to him on the other side of the projects just a half hour earlier. He hated to think about what just happened to him. Too bad his mind's eye couldn't shed tears and cleanse his thoughts.

Chapter 3

"Good morning, Tafari," Mahogany cheered. "So are you gonna meet me in front of my building so we can walk to school together?"

"Um, I can't," Tafari stammered, holding the phone with his right hand and holding his ribs with his left. "Um, I got something to do."

"Like what?"

"Um, something for my mom. I might even be a little late for school this morning. So you just go ahead and walk to school by yourself and I'll catch up with you later."

"I was really looking forward to us walking to school together. I hate walking through this block with all these thugs over here hanging out in front of my building. With you at my side, I would feel so safe." A lump the size of a jawbreaker swelled in Tafari's throat. As if he didn't already feel like less of a man after getting jumped about twenty yards away from Mahogany's building. *Did Mahogany really expect all five-foot-six, one hundred and forty pounds of me to protect her from the gangs of menacing thugs that hung around on her block? Girls can be so unreasonable,* Tafari thought. She had to see how those thugs were glaring at him when they were walking to Mahogany's building the previous night. As Tafari and Mahogany talked in the lobby with the thugs watching them, the tension in the air was thick enough to bite into. *She had to sense that.* If she did sense it and didn't say anything, then she was selfish and was only concerned about her own safety. And if she didn't sense it, then she was as naïve as he always thought she was.

"I wish I could be there for you, but like I said, I have to do something for Mom. I'm sure I'll see you between classes."

"Maybe we can meet up between third and fourth period class since we have third period class on the same floor."

"Okay. I'll see you after third period."

"Bye." Tafari hung up the house phone and tried to shake the sense of guilt that overcame him. He hated to lie, but he hated getting kicked in the ribs even more.

When Tafari left his apartment, he entered the staircase and took a seat on the top step and waited. He didn't want to risk the chance of running into Mahogany in school while walking to morning homeroom since he told her he was going to be late. After about a half hour, he exited his building, and for the first time, he was going to be tardy for school.

Tafari never saw the block so quiet. Just a few minutes earlier, the sidewalks were covered by hoards of mothers hand in hand with toddlers wearing colorful backpacks and middle and high school students who spilled in and out of the deli while making their way toward the schools. Some of the students darted in to the streets, zigzagging between a traffic jam of honking cars on their way to the nearest freeway to get to work.

And in a flash, the streets were deserted. *So this is what the streets are like when everyone is in school*, Tafari thought. No kids to dodge as they ran up and down the block playing, no pretty girls to try and then fail to impress, and most importantly, no thugs on the corners to hide from. It was so peaceful. For the first time, Tafari felt at ease outside of his window.

The sound of laughter and loud boasting ripped through the quiet block. Tafari's face cringed from the heat as he looked off into the distance. Three familiar figures bopped up the hill toward him. The closer they got, the larger they grew as if ascending from the ocean. Tafari recognized Lil' Headache, Stretch, and Los instantly. His nerves began to run amuck as if he was high on caffeine. Tafari wanted to turn and run, but then again he wasn't on the southside. He was on the northside. His side.

Tafari dropped his head and tried to circle around, but Lil' Headache stepped in his path. Half of Lil' Headache's hair was braided in cornrows, which were buried under a forest of loose strands, while the other half was picked out in a wild afro. Tafari glanced into Lil' Headache's stone face.

"Excuse me," Tafari said in a soft voice, barely above a whisper. He found himself surrounded by Stretch, a tall, wiry, light-skinned dude and Los, a short Puerto Rican boy.

"You live around here?" Lil' Headache snarled.

"Yeah," Tafari mumbled.

"Yo, Headache, chill. A cop car," Los warned. Lil' Headache turned toward the street. The cop car pulled up to the curb and chirped its siren.

"Shouldn't you boys be heading to school?" the cop asked from the driver's seat.

"We're on our way now. We were just stopping in the deli to get a bagel first," Lil' Headache answered. With their attention on the cop, Tafari managed to slip away unseen and took off running down the alley way between the deli and the laundromat. Tafari didn't stop running until he reached Bronx High.

"You're late," Mr. Sekou said to Tafari, who had just entered first period English. Tafari handed Mr. Sekou a tardy pass. Mr. Sekou took the pass but didn't bother to look at it. Instead, he studied Tafari's face. His eyes seemed to concentrate on a spot just above Tafari's eyes.

"Is everything alright, Tafari?" Mr. Sekou asked, worry in his voice. Tafari dropped his head. "Everything is fine."

"If you say so. Go take a seat." Tafari sat at the only tablet arm desk available in the front. He ran his index finger across his forehead and could feel the scratches and scrapes from hitting his head on the concrete when he got jumped the night before. "Okay class, as I was saying, take out your writer's notebooks," Mr. Sekou instructed. "Today's writing prompt is 'Should students be required to wear school uniforms?' You guys have fifteen minutes to brainstorm in your writer's notebooks. Before I set the timer, does anyone have a question or comment?"

"I have a comment," Sebastian Reyes called out from the back of the classroom.

"What's your comment, Sebastian?"

"No offense, but these prompts you be givin' us are lame. I mean, last week we had to write an essay convincing the teacher to 'allow students to chew gum in the classroom.' And now we have to write about 'school uniforms'? Nobody wants to write to these corny prompts. No offense."

"No offense taken, Sebastian," Mr. Sekou responded. "And by the way, you rarely come to school to write to these so-called *lame* prompts. So why do you even care? No offense." The class laughed. Sebastain glared at Mr. Sekou from the back of the room. "My classroom is an open forum where I allow you guys to express your opinions freely," Mr. Sekou said, turning to face the rest of the class. "Any other student feels as Sebastain does? Does anyone feel that the prompts I've been giving you are *lame* and *corny*?" Slowly, arms were rising into the air all across the room. After Mr. Sekou scanned the room, he tossed a stack of papers into the trash bin by the classroom door. "Since you guys don't like my prompts, I will allow you to create your own." Cheering and whistling erupted in the classroom. Mr. Sekou stood at the whiteboard with a dry-erase marker in his hand. "Alright, let's compile a list of possible prompts and we'll pick the best—"

"No need for a list," Timothy Morgan interrupted. "I already got a prompt idea that we can all relate to."

"And what's that, Timothy?"

"We should write about gangs."

"Gangs?" Sebastain called out. "I ain't writin' about no gang 'cause I ain't no snitch. And, Timothy, you don't know nothin' about no gangs anyway. You a lame."

"I ain't no lame!" Timothy shouted, standing up.

"Boy, you better sit down before you lay down!" Sebastian shouted back.

"Alright! Alright! That's enough! Both of you calm down! I will not have any shouting in my classroom."

"As I was saying," Timothy said, turning to Mr. Sekou. "What student in this classroom can't write about gangs? We see 'em everyday when we go home because they're all over the streets. They're all up in the projects—"

"And all over this school," Mr. Sekou added. Sebastian and some of the boys in the back arched their eyebrows in surprise. "You didn't think I knew about the gangs in this school? I'm not like most of the other teachers at this school that can't relate to their students and live way up in White Plains and Dobbs Ferry. I grew up in the projects just like you guys."

"Do you still live in the projects?" Timothy asked.

"No, I live in these co-op apartment buildings now. But it might as well be the projects with all the violence that's been occurring lately."

"So, what about gangs are we going to be writing about?" Imani Lewis inquired.

"Good question, Imani. Does anyone have a suggestion?"

"We can write about the history of it," Timothy called out.

"In order to write about the history of gangs, we would need to do some research first. And that would take longer than we have," Mr. Sekou reasoned.

"Research?" Sebastian called out. "We don't need to do no research. Everybody knows that gangs were started by Latinos and African Americans."

"That's not true," Mr. Sekou said, correcting Sebastian. "Actually, the history of gangs can be traced back to as early as the eighteenth century. Now, there were some black gangs during this time but the majority of gangs were white."

"There were white gangs?" Timothy wondered out loud.

"Absolutely. Like I said, the earliest known gangs can be traced all the way back to right after the American Revolution. The earliest modern day gangs in New York were largely Irish and this was in the early 1900s. When the Irish immigrated to the United States, they were very poor and starving, carrying everything they owned in bags, as was the case with all immigrants. Then right after that, there was the arrival of Italian immigrants who came over, and similar to the Irish immigrants, they were poor too. And soon after their arrival, Italian gangs started to emerge. While this is going on, poor Jewish immigrants arrived on Ellis Island and they too began their new lives in the slums of New York. And just like the other immigrants before them, Jewish gangs started to pop up on the scene."

Imani raised her hand, "It seems like all of the gangs came out of poor areas."

"Good observation, Imani," Mr. Sekou pointed out. "All of the immigrants were forced to live in filthy, crowded tenement houses that were supposed to be temporary but turned out to be permanent. And whenever you place a large concentration of starving people, regardless of skin color, in overcrowded, poverty-stricken, low-income buildings, unrest will emerge. Violence will emerge. Gangs will emerge."

"Most African Americans didn't migrate to the United States; they were brought over as slaves. So when did African Americans start to form their own gangs?" Timothy asked, curiosity bubbling in his eyes.

"Like I mentioned earlier, there were African American gangs here in the United States back in the 1800s. But the more modern gangs, especially in New York, can be traced back to the migration of southern African Americans who were seeking better job opportunities up here in the north. This was during the 1940s and 1950s. When African Americans migrated to the north, inter-racial conflicts began. Young white males started to form groups or gangs because they didn't want their neighbor-hoods integrated. As a way to protect themselves, African Americans formed their own groups which were known as brotherhoods. So as you can see, the brotherhood was formed to bring African Americans together. Nowadays, the brotherhood has given way to gangs. And we no longer fight for *the cause*. We fight *because*."

"So how did we end up in the projects?" Imani asked.

"The southern African Americans were just as poor as the immigrants who came over from Europe. Even though African Americas were already here, in the United States, we were slaves and owned by white people. When African Americans were freed, we weren't owned any longer, but we didn't own anything ourselves. So when African Americans went to the north looking for work, most of them settled in the low-income, poverty-stricken ghettos."

"Wow, I actually learned something in school today," Sebastian called out.

"Well, if you would come to school more often, you would learn a lot more," Mr. Sekou shot back.

"If we had more lessons like this that I could relate to, maybe I'd come to school more."

Mr. Sekou nodded. He turned to the rest of the class. "I must say the quality of writing from this class over the past few weeks has been on a sharp decline. But since you guys picked your own topic, hopefully I'll see some passion in your writing." Together, the class put together a prompt and began to brainstorm about 'the influences of gangs.' Based on what he had been through over the last twenty-four hours, Tafari had a bunch of ideas in his head, but the class conversation about gangs lasted so long, he really didn't have a chance to fully brainstorm on the paper. It was more of a light drizzle. But even after the bell rang and Tafari was off to his next class, the storm about gangs continued to brew in his head.

Chapter 4

Usually, Tafari was very aware of his surroundings, especially when he wasn't locked safely behind the iron door of apartment 6C. Whether he was going to or leaving from Bible study, Tafari made sure he scanned the area. His eyes would dart back and forth, frantically, like a trapped rat searching for an exit. Tafari could spot a gang of thugs who might present a problem with him getting home safely from about five street lights away. Even standing on a subway platform with a train whizzing by, his eyes would dip into each passing car window, searching for a safe one. Once he picked a car and took a seat, every now and then he would lean forward and peer through the glass of the car door to see if anyone was trying to get in to the car he was occupying.

But that night, his eyes were closed. Literally. With Mahogany's head laying on his shoulder and their fingers tangled, Tafari leaned back and closed his eyes. Tafari and Mahogany were on their way home from the teen rap session. Just like two nights before, Mahogany snuck out from under her mom's watchful eyes and met Tafari at the youth center. And just like two nights before, they stopped at the Jamaican restaurant and bought another pan of jerk chicken. Not for Mahogany's uncle, but for Mahogany. Her uncle let her sample jerk chicken for the first time and Mahogany was hooked by the sweet heat of the spicy dark meat.

While Mahogany was stewing in her own thoughts, Tafari stewed in a pool of worry. There was no way he could risk his life by walking Mahogany home again, he thought. But how would he get out of it? What could he say to her that would let him off the hook from having to walk her home and, at the same time, won't make him look like a punk in her eyes? Tafari had five stops to come up with an answer.

The sound of the car door dragging open and banging shut made Tafari's eyes pop open. Without turning his head, Tafari's eyes darted toward the direction of the noise. Kenroy Davis, who everyone on the streets and in school called Dready, and a big dude wearing a Mets hat were bopping toward them. Tafari didn't know Dready personally, but he definitely knew who he was. Anyone who knew what was *real* in the streets, or who attended

Bronx High, *knew* who he was. Mahogany obviously didn't. She offered him a half-innocent smile, as a greeting, while he approached ice-grillin' them. Tafari wished he were as naïve as she was, but he wasn't. Neither was his heart. It fluttered as he approached.

Tafari dropped his head and eyed his scuffed-up shoes trying to avoid looking directly at the flickering flames that burned in Dready's narrow eyes. He silently prayed that Dready would just bop on by. Dready had a rep of being a young wild thug that would do anything to anybody at anytime. Most of the thugs in the projects and in school were afraid of Dready.

Tafari's head remained down as Dready and Met-Hat bopped in front of them. But Tafari's eyes had to get one glimpse of him. He wanted to get an up close and personal look at the thug everyone was afraid of. Tafari saw him a few times in school whenever Dready decided to show up but never that close up.

With his head still down, Tafari's lifted his eyes towards Dready, slowly. Dready's face was the color of a Phillie blunt cigar. Loose strands of knotted up hair spread across his cheeks and jaw line, which would soon fill into a full knotty beard. Long, knotted up, dirty blonde dreadlocks grew from under his oversized green Jets hat.

Tafari glanced at him no longer than one second, if that long. Dready stopped his bop. So did Met-Hat. So did Tafari's heart. That quick glance was all it took for that short-fused dude to detonate. "Why ya look 'pon me?!" Dready barked, his voice seasoned with a Jamaican accent.

Mahogany's innocent smile melted away and the flicker her eyes usually carried went dim. The usual internal light that gave her an external glow was blown out by her first encounter with the streets. She gave Tafari's fingers a squeeze, wanting him to make it all go away, but there was nothing he could do.

Just minutes earlier, when Tafari and Mahogany stepped onto the train, there were three people already occupying seats. Tafari scanned the car, looking for help or a witness to what was about to go down when he realized he and Mahogany would have to fend for themselves against Dready and Met-Hat. The passengers must have vacated their seats while Tafari had his eyes closed. Or, they had their own set of spidey senses and fled to another train car when they saw Dready and Met-Hat making their way into their train car.

"I said why ya look 'pon me?!" Dready barked, again.

"I . . . um . . . I wasn't—" Tafari stammered, searching for words.

"Yo, gimme a blood-clot dollar!"

"I don't have any money."

"What! Stand up!"

Tafari obeyed the order and rose to a slumped stance. His heart tried to kick a hole in his chest. Tafari's head remained down and his eyes stayed away from Dready's.

But his eyes couldn't stay off of the bling-blinging golden medallion that hung from his Cuban link chain.

"Yo, him look like a scared choir bwoy," Dready joked with Met-Hat. While chuckling at his joke, Dready stuck his hand in Tafari's front pocket and fished out a hand full of change.

"Thought ya said ya haf no money? Ya lie t' me?"

"Nah . . . I . . . um . . . I didn't know," Tafari said, nearly hyperventilating. Dready grabbed Tafari by his collar and reeled him in. "Me nah like de way ya face look," Dready growled, studying Tafari's face. "Why ya look like dat?"

"I don't know. I was just born like this," Tafari apologized.

"Yo bredren," Dready turned to Met-Hat. "Dis looks like dat bwoy dat pushed ya brotha 'pon de train tracks last year." Met-Hat moved in on Tafari. He got so close to Tafari, the brim of his hat stabbed him in the forehead, and when Met-Hat spoke, it smelled like someone took a dump in his mouth. Tafari's nose cringed as Met-Hat sneered, "You the one who pushed my brother onto the train tracks?"

"Nah, that wasn't me. I swear." Tafari put his right hand up to show he was telling the truth. He even thought about removing the Bible from his backpack and putting his left hand on it.

Dready reached for the bag of jerk chicken that sat on the seat next to Mahogany. He dipped his nose in the bag and glared at Tafari. "Ya got food and ya nah offer me and my bredren, Donovan, any? I should box ya in ya face." Dready balled up his left fist and flinched as if he were going to punch Tafari. Tafari threw his arms over his face and stumbled into a seat. Dready and Donovan laughed at his clumsiness.

"Yo bredren, ya hungry?" Dready asked Donovan.

"Starvin'!" Dready tossed the greasy paper bag of jerk chicken to Donovan. He reached into the bag and pulled out the aluminum pan. Donovan took a seat next to Mahogany, popped off the white paper top and grabbed a handful of rice and peas and stuffed his mouth.

"Hey, that's mine!" Mahogany insisted.

"Shut up! It's mine now!" Donovan yelled, rice and peas spraying out of his mouth. "And next time buy some soda or something. I'm chokin' over here." His uneven teeth tore into a chicken leg. Mahogany glared at him. Her eyes were saying things Tafari was sure she never fixed her mouth to say before.

"Chill, chill bredren. De gal kinda cute," Dready said to Donovan. Dready approached Mahogany, his red eyes were wide and his mouth was twisted into a crooked smile. "I apologize on behaf of me brethren. Him nah know how t' talk t' de ladies propaly. But ya see me? Me know how t' talk t' de ladies and make dem feel good, ya know? So t' accept me apology is t' accept me kiss." Dready poked out his ashy lips and leaned toward Mahogany's face. She reached out with two open palms and tried with all her might to hold him off. Veins were pulsing from her neck as she pushed on his chest but Dready was too strong. His crusty lips sliced across her mouth before he flashed a crooked-tooth smile.

The light on Mahogany's face went dull when Dready first approached them, but after the unexpected kiss, a new light rekindled. A twinkling dark one.

Mahogany looked like she wanted to strike Dready, but her arms were pinned by her side. She stopped struggling and cocked her neck back like the hammer on a pistol. It sprung forward and her mouth fired foamywhite, thick saliva onto Dready's smile.

Dready cursed and jumped back, wiping his mouth with his right hand. He opened his left palm and smashed Mahogany across her right cheek. Smacked her so hard strings of tears lept from between her eyelids. Tafari's arm reacted before his mind knew what happened. Reaching out with his right hand, he grabbed Dready's arm and pulled him away from Mahogany. Dready whirled around and shoved Tafari against the train door. He reached for his waist and pulled out an old black gun with a duct-taped handle. It looked like it would have fallen apart if his finger squeezed the trigger. Dready aimed it at Tafari's nose anyway. Tafari's heart almost collapsed and his bladder caved in and tried to empty.

"Why ya gon put ya hands 'pon me fa?!" Dready shouted. "Huh?! Ya wan' dead? Ya must wan' dead!" This time, Tafari's bladder succeeded. Just a little bit, though.

"Ya touch me clothes now I take yours," Dready continued. "Strip off de choir bwoy clothes, now!" Just as he threatened Tafari, the train came to a stop. Silently, Tafari prayed for someone, anyone, to get on. If someone tried to get on the train, they probably wouldn't have made it. It seemed like the train doors closed shut as soon as they dragged open.

"I said strip off de pants, mon!" Dready commanded. Tafari glanced at Mahogany, whose face was buried in her hands. Her body jerked every other second as if she had the hiccoughs. She kept sniffling, too. It was obvious that she was crying, but what wasn't so obvious is, was she crying because she was humiliated by Dready or by Tafari?

Tafari knew for a fact that he was humiliated by himself. Dready and Donovan had a lot to do with it but it was Mahogany who had the most to do with it. If she wasn't there on the train and Tafari was by himself with Dready aiming a gun at him and Donovan was eating his food, and he was able to survive and get off the train alive, he could take that scene on the train and bury it deep in the well of his mind. Just like he buried the scene on the southside deep within. Tafari would convince himself that it never happened and would never tell anyone. Especially not Mahogany. And she would have never seen that side of him.

Without hesitation, Tafari loosened his belt, kicked off his shoes, and dropped his pants. The gun moved up to his chest and waved for him to remove his suit jacket, tie, and white shirt. Tafari stood before the old gun in a pair of tight, white boxers with blue squares on them and a pair of black dress socks that reached just below his ashy calves.

The train came to a screeching halt, one stop before Tafari and Mahogany's stop. Dready balled up Tafari's clothes in one arm and tucked his gun back into his waist. A brown-skinned lady in a blue business suit was revealed when the doors dragged open. *Where in the world was she one stop ago?* Tafari thought. *I might still have my clothes on had she gotten on the stop before. And I might still have my dignity had she gotten on three stops earlier.* The lady hesitated to get on when she saw Tafari cowering in his boxers. But her presence at the door was enough to startle Dready and Donovan.

"Layta, rude bwoy," Dready remarked, brushing by Tafari. Donovan followed Dready through the door with Mahogany's pan of jerk chicken in his hands. Dready dumped Tafari's clothes onto the train tracks just before the train pulled off.

Tafari took a seat next to Mahogany, who still hid her face with her hands. Without looking, she handed Tafari her black trench coat and he wrapped the too-small coat around his cold body. Neither one of them said anything for the rest of the ride. Tafari couldn't bring himself to lift his eyes in Mahogany's direction. He was afraid to.

When they got off the train, they went their separate ways. Mahogany couldn't bring herself to look at Tafari before she turned and walked away. Tafari decided to walk the long way home. The long way being the not-too-pop-ulated-by-too-many-people way. He didn't notice anyone noticing him except for a group of girls who stopped their loud chatter to size him up from his dress socks, to his tight trench, all the way up to his red, watery eyes. They exploded with laughter just as Tafari crept by them and entered the building.

Tafari clutched his keys in his fist to prevent them from jingling when he unlocked the apartment door. He stood in the doorway and listened. Just like two nights ago, his mom was in her bedroom, probably watching the Cosby Show. Tafari was able to slip in his bedroom unseen.

After slipping into a T-shirt and basketball shorts, he dried his eyes with the back of his hand and took a seat on the radiator facing the window. Tafari's eyes were as useful as a pair of binoculars with no one behind them peering through the lenses. He wasn't seeing because *he* wasn't behind his eyes. He was still on that train with Mahogany. But she wasn't with him. There was nobody behind her binoculars, either. Mahogany's stare was dis-tant and Tafari was sure somewhere behind that distant stare, Mahogany was in there, questioning how she could have fallen for a coward like him.

Noise from the street corner made Tafari scramble behind his ebony binoculars. He looked down and saw Lil' Headache, Stretch, and Los chillin' on the corner. Tafari wondered to himself if Lil' Headache, Stretch, and

Los's rep was big enough to scare someone like Dready. If Tafari had a rep like them, he doubted that incident with Dready would have ever gone down. If he had one, he doubted he would have let Dready undress him the way he did. And if he had one, Mahogany wouldn't have had to bury her face in her hands from embarrassment. The problem was, he had to figure out how to get a rep just like those thugs on the corner.

Chapter 5

About a week to the day after he undressed in front of Dready and his old thirty-eight with Dready standing behind it, Tafari put on an outfit that mirrored the uniform of the menacing dreadlocked thug. A pair of black jeans, a black hooded sweatshirt, and a pair of tan, suede Timberlands. The inner thug that often hid behind his eyes appeared before him in the mirror and tried on the similar intimidating masks and scowls that Dready wore on the train.

"How do I look?" Tafari asked, turning to the twins.

"Like one of them thugs on the corner," Leon admitted. "If I didn't know you and I saw you on the corner I might be too shook to walk past you. I might have to cross the street and circle around you."

"Fareal?" Tafari wondered.

"Yeah, but why did you buy that outfit?"

"Like I told y'all earlier, I think the main reason why I got jumped on the southside and robbed on the train is because of the dress clothes my mother always makes me wear. The dress clothes that I wear are like a billboard with one message: *If you are a thug or gang member, please come rob or jump me.*" Tafari and the twins laughed together. Tafari continued, "I figured if I wear an outfit like this, I can at least blend in."

"Where did you get the money to buy those Timbs and the clothes?" Leon wondered.

"I been saving up my allowance." Tafari's locked doorknob shook and rattled as if someone was trying to get in. He stumbled away from the mirror, fumbling with the top button of his jeans. Mom had no idea that her son was on the other side of his locked bedroom door trying on the same outfit as the thugs she saw in the lobby on her way home from work and would call the cops on for loitering as soon as she got in the apartment.

"Tafari, the phone!" Mom called out from the hall. Tafari's jeans sagged to his ankles and he penguin-walked the rest of the way to his bed.

"Who is it?"

"It's Mahogany."

"Um, just tell her I left already."

"I'm tired of lying for you, Tafari. This is the last time. What's going on with y'all two anyway? You've been dodging her phone calls all week."

"Just don't wanna speak to her right now."

"This is the last time," Mom reminded.

Tafari glanced at the twins. "It's a good thing I locked that door. If my mother walked in here she would make me strip just like Dready made me strip a week ago."

"Yeah, but unlike Dready, she wouldn't have been standing in front of you with a gun; she would have had Betty Sue in her hands," Noel laughed.

"Yeah," Leon added. "And unlike Dready, ya mom would have used her weapon of choice right across the back of ya legs." The twins laughed.

"Whatcha'll know about Betty Sue?" Tafari quizzed.

"My mother told us that Betty Sue is an old leather belt that was older than you. And one time when we got in trouble, our mom borrowed Betty Sue from your mom and introduced us." Leon winced from the memories, rubbing the back of his leg.

"Y'all are crazy."

"Why have you been dodging Mahogany's calls? I thought y'all were goin' out now?" Noel asked.

"I don't know what to say to her. And I'm not sure I'm ready to hear what she has to say to me, either."

"Because of what happened on the train?"

"Yeah. When Dready and Donovan punked me in front of her. Made me feel like less of a man in front of her even though I'm not a man yet, but y'all know what I mean. I just can't face her right now."

"But didn't y'all see each other at church this past Sunday?"

"Nah. I played sick. I told Mom I wasn't feeling well and she let me stay home. She was really upset because we usually get there early so I can help set up the youth service. Plus, Mahogany doesn't attend our church anymore so I doubt she was there."

Ms. Green called to Leon and Noel and they left Tafari's room. Tafari changed his clothes and stuffed his new thug uniform into his backpack before he grabbed his rhyme book and flipped it open to the first page which was the first rhyme he ever wrote in that book.

His eyes slid across the blue lines and fed each word to his mouth, reciting the lyrics in his head. Smiled and laughed as if his tongue never spit the shocking similes before. Still pictures of the actual day that he penned the rhymes he was reciting flashed in his mind. For each page that he turned, another picture would pop up in his mind like a photo album.

Finally, he landed on the last page that he actually wrote on. Tafari had been working on that rhyme for about a week. Just couldn't put the pencil down. Couldn't keep from erasing and starting over and rewriting punch lines until they were tight. He finally finished the rhyme earlier that afternoon in boring chemistry class. It was a whole page. Front and back. When Tafari finally put the pencil down, his eyes continued to stroke the lyrical masterpiece on the papermate canvas. He couldn't believe it was his hand that wrote it. It was by far the hardest, most street-thuggish rhyme he ever wrote in that book.

Tafari stuffed his rhyme book in his backpack and he was dressed and ready for Bible study in less than two minutes. He usually headed for the elevator and pressed the down button once he left the apartment, but on that evening, he took the stairs and went up to the roof. That was the first time he ever stepped foot on the bed of tar lined with millions of tiny pebbles. The sun hovered so close to the roof, Tafari felt as if he could reach out and touch it. He moved a few paces out onto the roof, dropped his backpack, squatted to one knee, and removed the jeans, the sweatshirt, and Timberlands. As quickly as he could, Tafari stripped off the Bible study outfit and replaced it with his new thug uniform.

Hurrying across the pebbles, Tafari slid to a stop just before he reached out for the doorknob. He thought he heard voices on the other side of the door. Tafari placed his ear to the door and he could hear someone rapping. In the background, someone was doing a horrible Doug-E-Fresh beat-box impersonation. Tafari had to listen carefully to hear the rhyme.

Lil' Headache's the name

I'm out for the fame

mess wit me, I'll put you to shame

when I pull out my gun

yo, you better run

'cause gettin' hit by hot shells ain't no fun.

Tafari snickered because he couldn't believe someone with such a thugged-out gangster reputation like Lil' Headache would kick some ole cat-'n-the-hat nursery rhyme like that. As Tafari moved closer to get a better listen to the non-competition, his Timberlands slid out from under him. Tafari reached out and grabbed the door handle to keep from falling, but the weight of his body slammed against the door. All of a sudden, the music stopped on the other side of the door.

Actually, everything seemed to stop. Including his brain. It froze up and didn't suggest any ways to escape. When it finally started to thaw out a few seconds later, it did offer one suggestion. Told him to run. Tafari attempted to, until the rest of his brain completely thawed out and told him how stupid he must have looked, running around in circles on the roof, looking for a place to hide. Only one place to hide on that roof and it was six floors down. If the rest of his brain didn't thaw out when it did, he might have jumped over the edge and hid.

The door inched open. Everything stopped again. Everything except for the door. Lil' Headache, Stretch, and Los appeared in the doorway, each one of them with their eyebrows and mouths frowned and their eyes slit in anger, staring through Tafari. Lil' Headache was the first to step onto the sheet of pebbles. As Lil' Headache took another step toward him, Tafari's Timberlands took one step backwards. His brain froze again.

"Whatchu doin' up here, yo? This is my roof!" Lil' Headache snapped. Tafari's brain was still thawing out, so it didn't offer any suggestions. Lil' Headache had taken another black-Timberland step toward Tafari. A scowl was chiseled on his stone face. "I said, whatchu doin' on my roof?!" Lil' Headache repeated.

"Yo, let's throw him off the roof!" Los shouted.

"Ain't that that kid we was about to rob last week?" Stretch asked.

"Yeah, it sure is," Lil' Headache said, studying Tafari's face. "Five-0 saved you last week but ain't nobody up here to save you. Time to empty those pockets."

Tafari was desperate. He had to do something to rescue himself from yet another beat down. His mouth reached out and grabbed a hold of the first thought, the only thought that had been circulating his brain since chemistry earlier in the afternoon. Tafari's tongue took over from there.

Corner thugs be stackin' crack funds

and blastin' guns

snitches caught flappin' their gums

get jumped and pumped wit' holes and dumped in the back of the slums

a thugs trigger finger stay itchin'

hittin' enemies wit' red laser beam precision

leavin' victims in a ditch and

they'll be half dead and twitchin'

that's life on the corner

remorseless thugs quick to extinguish the light in ya cornea

the front bench of a funeral parlor will be packed tight wit' mourners

project mothers are often

crouched over coffins

awkward

cryin' and coughin'

mournin' in

morbid, funeral homes wit' their sons layin' dormant

the crime was tragic

these streets resemble national geographic

ghetto wildlife, they handle beef not with claws or teeth but wit' plastic, glock automatics

these thugs are concrete jungle predators

they'll become ya autobiography movie editors

rip you out of ya own script, changin' victims endin's on the regular

that's not the way you was supposed to die

a fourteen-year-old' corpse layin' in the gutter wit' open eyes . . .

Tafari's rhyme wasn't finished but his breath was. He couldn't continue. Tafari was hunched over with his mouth and nostrils flared trying to catch the dry roof air. Since that was the first time he had ever rhymed in front of anyone before, Tafari figured it was nerves that sucked the air from his lungs.

"That rhyme was *tight*. Yo, you mad nice, son," Stretch reacted first.

"Yo, Headache, this little dude would eat you in a battle, yo," Los remarked, laughing with Stretch.

"Get outta here, man. That couldn't have been his rhyme," Lil' Headache said, not wanting to believe it. "That rhyme sounded like a hot rapper wit' a record deal or somethin'."

"Nah, that was mine. I wrote it myself. Fareal," Tafari answered.

"*That* was really ya rhyme?"

"Yeah."

"Dag, man, how you think of stuff like that?" Lil' Headache asked, staring at Tafari in awe.

"I don't know. When my pen hits the paper, I just zone out." Tafari shrugged.

"Yo, he said, 'leavin' victims in a ditch and they'll be half dead and twitchin',"' Stretch chuckled. "Yo, that line was mad ill."

"What's ya name?" Lil' Headache asked.

"Tafari."

"You live around here?"

"Yeah, I live in this building."

"How come I ain't ever seen you around here before?"

"I don't really be hangin' around here."

"So where you hang at?"

"Nowhere really. I just be in the crib, writin' rhymes."

"I believe you, too," Stretch admitted. "You gotta be in the crib for a while, writin' for a long time to rhyme like *that*. That rhyme you kicked sounds better than all of that stuff I hear on the radio."

"Good lookin', man," Tafari thanked.

That was all it took. On the strength of that one rhyme, Tafari was accepted. Night after night, Tafari would sit six floors up with his face pressed against the window bars, staring at the corner. Tafari's mind's eye had no way of seeing that the rhymes he scribbled in his rhyme book would be his pass to pose in front of the deli with the rest of the thugs that crowded the corner.

Tafari's window overlooked people with similar names, looks, and wants. Only a chosen few were able to stand out amongst the overcrowded. Some had a nice jump shot like Stretch and others had a nice knuckle game like Lil' Headache and could knuckle down just about anybody regardless of size. The rest, like Los, would do anything at any time to prove they were just as crazy as the next man in the projects. Then you had people like Tafari. He became known as the kid who was nice with the rhymes.

After Tafari spit those hot rhymes on the roof, they headed for the deli. Across the street from Tafari's build-ing were an endless number of blocks tied together by countless strip malls that surrounded the projects. The deli was on the end of the first block. Right next to the deli was a check cashing place, a laundromat, liquor store, Mario's pizza shop, and Lee's Kitchen on the end. About four blocks down, the middle and high schools wedged in between the strip malls.

Tafari was tucked between his new friends, frozen in their thug poses, crowding the entrance of the deli. With his thug outfit on and the scowl that masked his face, Tafari blended in with the thugs like camouflage. The scene reminded Tafari of something one of the boys in the locker room once said about living in the projects. The boy said, "As a young man growing up in the projects, you were either a predator or you were prey." Tafari was now rubbing shoulders with the street corner predators, watching the prey cower down the street, scared to look in the eyes of Tafari and his new crew on the corner. As Tafari observed some of the boys walk with their heads down and others crossing the street, afraid to walk across the path of Tafari and his crew, he was reminded of himself. Reminded of the time when he was the prey.

But even though he was down with the predators, Tafari's body was jittery as if he was cold. It wasn't the constant gust of the wind that gave him chill bumps. It was nerves and curious excitement that rumbled in his gut like a blender. Tafari had proven to them that he was nice with the rhymes but he didn't prove to them that he was a thug. The fact that some old beef could just jump off at any time on the corner had Tafari feeling a little uneasy. But he still looked up at his window as if he was looking for his face pressed on the glass. If only he could see himself on the corner.

Chapter 6

The next morning, Tafari had just exited his building on his way to school when Lil' Headache, Stretch, and Los approached him.

"Whassup, bruh. Where ya goin'?" Lil' Headache asked.

"I'm on my way to school."

"School? Nah, man, come chill with us."

"Chill witch'all? Doin' what?"

"Just kickin' it."

"You mean, play hooky from school?"

"No doubt. School is lame. We about to go get some snacks from the deli, then we gonna chill in Los's apartment and play video games. So, you in or what?"

Lil' Headache's words were an open invitation to be officially down with them. Tafari never played hooky a day in his life but he knew he had to accept the invitation.

If he turned down the invite, they probably would have robbed him on the spot, beat him down, and sent him back behind his window, cowering because he was too shook to ever walk that block again. Tafari shivered at the thought of being stuck behind his window.

"I'm down," Tafari declared. As soon as Tafari spoke those words, a familiar silver jeep crept slowly up the street. A jeep that looked just like Ms. Green's. It pulled up at the curb just down the block. Tafari burst through the entrance of the deli and hid behind the potato chip rack, which was shoved up against the window. Tafari moved stacks of chips to either side, clearing a lane for his eyes to penetrate the dingy glass. He silently prayed that Ms. Green didn't see him.

Lil' Headache, Stretch, and Los entered behind him.

"You okay?" Los asked, tapping Tafari on the shoulder.

"Yeah. I'm good."

"You sure? Because you came flying in here like ya running from someone."

"Oh, yeah. Um . . . I thought I saw a cop."

"Fareal? Where?"

"Um . . . he's gone now."

"Good." It was a typical Bronx deli: A counter in the front with a wall of bulletproof glass separating the cashier from the patrons. A box-sized cutout in the glass, just enough space for the cashier to poke his head out and watch them browse. Behind the bulletproof glass on a shelf were boxes of cigarettes, cigars, Swisher Sweets, and mixtape CDs. Lil' Headache, Stretch, and Los went straight to the cupcake racks, stacked against the stained glass just to the left of the entrance. Just beside the snack rack were shelves of potato chips, pretzels, and popcorn. Straight to the back was a high counter with a meat slicer on top, and just below the counter behind thick glass were hunks of ham, turkey, roast beef, and cheeses. Tafari could recall many times when he strolled to the back of the deli and ordered turkey and Swiss cheese heros when Mom didn't feel like cooking that night.

Lil' Headache, Stretch, and Los each grabbed a pack of Butterscotch Krimpets from the snack rack and headed to the counter to pay. Tafari couldn't believe thugs actually ate Tastey Kakes. He used to buy a pack almost every day after school. *So, I do have something in common with thugs*, Tafari thought.

Before leaving the deli, Tafari's eyes cut in every direction until he was sure the jeep was gone. They spent the rest of the school day in Los's apartment, playing video games in his room and raiding his refrigerator. After three o'clock, they went back outside and chilled at the bus stop just as school let out.

"Yo, yo, ma. C'mere, lemme holla atchu for a minute!" Lil' Headache called out at a group of girls who were strutting by. Girls were hopping, skipping, and dancing from the reach of Lil' Headache's grasp as he tried to reel them in to his crew of wolves at the bus stop. Other girls picked up the pace of their strut when they saw the wolf pack. They winced and even ducked their heads from Lil' Headache, Stretch, and Los's comments as if they were being stoned by their words.

A group of butter-pecan-face Puerto Rican girls made their way toward the bus stop. And they were literally a group, smashed together as if they were joined at the hips.

"Yo, how you say that phrase in Spanish again?" Lil' Headache nudged Los.

"What phrase?"

"Remember, you were teaching me how to say something in Spanish. I forgot—"

"Oh, you mean *give me a kiss*."

"Yeah, yeah, yeah. How you say that?"

"Dame beso." Lil' Headache cleared his throat and stepped out from the bus stop.

"Mommies! Hey, mommies!" Lil' Headache called out to the Puerto Rican triplets. All six eyes curiously glanced over at them. "Ven aqui! Mommies, ven aqui!" Lil' Headache continued. They laughed and snickered into their cuffed hands.

"Ven aqui! Dame beso!" The snickers erupted into laughter and they took off running across the street. Lil' Headache took a few steps toward them with his arms extended as if waiting for a hug. "Mi Amor! Mi Amor! Ven aqui!" Tafari could still see them laughing as they disappeared in the midst of bodies across the street.

Not all of the girls ran from Lil' Headache. A bronze-faced girl with a head full of wild extension braids flashed her metal braces at Lil' Headache. Tafari could tell by the look in her eyes that she knew him. Or knew of him. And his rep. She slowed down her strut, as if waiting for him to approach her.

Most of the young girls in the projects were ghetto star struck, Tafari admitted to himself. They wanted to be seen with one of the thugs with the biggest reps. And there weren't too many thugs on the northside of the projects with a bigger rep than Lil' Headache.

Lil' Headache met the girl halfway and whispered some slick playa lines in her ear. He whipped out his cell phone and entered the girl's number. She wandered off smiling and Lil' Headache bopped toward his crew bragging, "Got them digits. Y'all better step y'all game up. I'm in the lead one to zero." Tafari realized instantly that they were having a contest to see who could get the most phone numbers.

After about twenty minutes, Lil' Headache, Stretch, and Los were huddled together with their phones out, counting the numbers they secured. Tafari stood idly by, with his phone still secure in his pocket. None of the girls that walked by gave him a phone number or even a second look. It didn't matter though, Tafari thought. He still had Mahogany. At least he hoped he still did.

"Look at all these new phone numbers I got. I won! I'm the man! I'm the man!" Lil' Headache boasted, waving his phone in the air. Stretch and Los sucked their teeth and waved him off. Lil' Headache stopped in the middle of his boasting when he spotted three boys riding bikes on the other side of the street. Lil' Headache, Stretch, and Los shared a look. A look that only they could read. Before Tafari knew what was going on, Lil' Headache, Stretch, and Los took off running across the street. By the time Tafari caught up, they had already formed a circle around the boys on the bikes.

"Yo, let me get a ride on ya bike!" Lil' Headache demanded, gripping the handle bars of the red bike.

"I . . . I can't. I gotta get home before it gets too late," the boy on the bike stammered.

"I'll be right back, man. I'm just going to the store." With his body, Lil' Headache nudged the boy off the seat and took control of the bike. Stretch and Los did the same with the other two bikes. "Tafari, hop on the back," Lil' Headache ordered. Tafari hopped onto the huge pegs screwed onto the axle of the bike's back wheel. They were big enough for Tafari to stand on with his hands resting on Lil' Headache's shoulders. The bike swerved a bit as Lil' Headache pedaled and tried to balance the weight on the back. The boys stood on the curb and helplessly watched their bikes descend down the hill and vanish in the maze of buildings.

Lil' Headache, Stretch, and Los raced their bikes across the sidewalk as if death was coming for them. As if he was hot on the heels of their faded tan Timberlands. Tafari twisted and turned on the pegs to see if the boys they stole the bikes from were following them. The only thing following Tafari was the sun.

"You need ya own bike," Lil' Headache said to Tafari.

"There goes one right there," Los pointed, pedaling beside them.

"Let's go get it," Lil' Headache urged. They raced the bikes across the basketball court toward a boy on a silver Mongoose. Lil' Headache squeezed the hand brakes. Tafari jumped off the pegs as Lil' Headache's Timberlands slid off the pedals and hit the cracked pavement. The red bike leaned under the arch of Lil' Headache's legs. Stretch and Los pulled up beside them and circled around the boy on the Mongoose. Tafari's heart boomed in his chest when the boy on the bike turned around. He recognized the boy's face from church on Sundays.

"We gon' need to borrow ya bike for a while, lil' man," Lil' Headache demanded.

"My mom said she don't want nobody riding my bike," the boy pleaded, quietly. The short boy appeared to be shrinking by the second under the menacing glares of Lil' Headache, Stretch, and Los. Fear flickered in his eyes. Tafari imagined his eyes were similar to the boy's eyes when *he* was cowering in front of Dready's gun and when *he* was surrounded by the thugs on the southside. Tafari was feeling sorry for the boy but did his best to conceal his feelings from his new crew. He also tried his best to conceal his face from the boy. Tafari hid just behind Los's shoulder.

"Ya mother ain't out here. How would she know?"

"I . . . I just can't."

"I ain't askin' you, I'm tellin' you! Give up the bike! My homie needs a ride!" Lil' Headache pointed at Tafari. Los stepped aside revealing Tafari's face to the boy. A blanket of relief smothered the flames of fear in the boy's eyes. It was obvious to Tafari that the boy recognized him, too. Tafari had to do something before the boy blew his cover. The boy's eyes pleaded to Tafari for help. Then his mouth moved. Tafari figured he was about to say something that would tip off his new crew that he and the boy knew each other.

Tafari moved with the speed of an actual mongoose. He darted at the boy and shoved him by his chest. The boy stumbled backwards, bouncing off the back wheel and slamming onto the pavement. Quickly, Tafari jumped on the bike seat. "Come on, let's go!" Tafari urged. The silver Mongoose took off across the basketball court like a silver comet with Lil' Headache, Stretch, and Los zooming closely behind like the comet's tail.

***

The first coat of darkness draped itself over the red brick buildings. Tafari went upstairs to his apartment as he normally would after school, ate, changed, and then left at five to rejoin his new crew on the corner. According to Tafari's worn leather watch, he should have been on the train sitting next to Mahogany on his way to Bible study, but according to Lil' Headache, it was time for something else. "Yo, I'm thirsty. Who's down for some beer?"

"You know I'm down, dawg," Stretch answered.

"You ain't even gotta ask me. I'm always down," Los added.

"A'ight then. Ante up, punks. Whoever doesn't chip in ain't gettin' any of the beer. Not even a sip," Lil' Headache announced. Stretch and Los reached into their pockets at the same time and each of them placed a wrinkled dollar in Lil' Headache's open palm. They all turned to Tafari and the look they gave him was an invitation to drink with them.

Tafari never drank beer a day in his life, but he knew he had to accept the invitation. After playing hooky and stealing bikes with them, he was officially down so it was too late to turn back now.

Tafari looked up at his bare bedroom window. No one had their face pressed on the glass looking out, but for the first time, someone was on the other side of the window, on the corner, looking in. His eyes crawled a few windows to the left of his and he saw the twin's faces peeking through the window bars. They stared at Tafari in opened-mouth amazement. Just to the left of Twins' window, Mrs. Prier was in her bedroom window. From one sun to the next one, she was always in that window. Just watching. As always, her chin rested in the palm of her hand which was propped up by her elbow. Her portly face was as still as a photo as if the window served as her own personal picture frame.

"You down or what?" Lil' Headache asked, a sense of annoyance in his voice because Tafari was moving too slow. Tafari reached into his pocket, pulled out three dollars, and added it to the pile. "Five dollars?! That's it?!" Lil' Headache snapped, before adding two singles of his own. " Y'all a bunch of broke deadbeats. I wanted to get a six pack but we only have enough to buy an old school forty ounce. When we get it, don't be greedy. Two sips and pass."

They parked the bikes just outside the deli and followed Lil' Headache in.

"Whassup, Papi?" Lil' Headeach cheered, placing the forty-ounce bottle of beer on the counter along with the money. Papi, a red-skinned Spanish man with a salt and pepper mustache snatched the beer from the countertop and placed it behind him. "You come in here all de time and I tell you de same thing. I no sell beer to minors," Papi said in a heavy Spanish accent.

"Come on, Papi. There ain't any cops in here."

"You gonna buy something else or what?"

"As much candy as I buy in here. As much of my money as I give you, you can't do me this one solid? Yo, forget you, man!"

"Get outta my store, now!" Papi demanded. Lil' Headache whirled around and stomped toward the middle aisle. He grabbed the snack rack with both hands and rocked it back and forth until bags of potato chips and popcorn and pretzels were snowing into the aisle. Lil' Headache gave the rack one last big shove. It tipped over and crashed onto the shelves of the aisle in front of it, scattering rows of cans onto the floor.

Papi emerged from behind the bulletproof glass holding a Louisville Slugger high above his head. Lil' Headache was the first to turn and burst through the door. Tafari, Stretch, and Los chased after him. They jumped on their bikes and raced to the end of the block. Papi and his Louisville Slugger ended the chase at the door of his store.

"Yo, we gotta find somebody old enough to buy our beer for us," Lil' Headache suggested.

It was after five and a lot of somebodies old enough to buy their beer for them began stepping onto the block. Men with greasy faces and hands and dingy jumpers emerged from underneath cars and stepped foot onto the block. As did men in tight business suits with suitcases swinging from their fingers and men with wrinkled faces and khakis to match and lottery tickets tucked in their fists and younger dudes with sagging blue jeans and Timberlands. All of them were stepping onto the block from all angles. They all met up at the liquor store and were squeezing by each other in and out of the entrance. Some emerged from the entrance with brown paper bags in the shape of liquor bottles and disappeared into the night. Others sat on crates in front of the liquor store and poured brown liquids from the brown paper bags into plastic cups. They would sip, laugh, and watch as darkness ate away at the remaining pieces of daylight.

Lil' Headache asked an older teen who was wearing a Knicks hat to buy the beer for them. He was in and out of the store within a minute. He handed Lil' Headache the beer and kept the change. It wasn't much but he kept it. Lil' Headache decided they were going to drink in his building.

Lil' Headache lived in a high-rise building which was twelve floors as opposed to six floors in the low-rise buildings. The building lobby was dim and claustrophobic with what looked like hundreds of silver mailboxes lined on the walls to the right. Straight ahead was an orange elevator door.

They stepped onto the elevator and took it all the way up to the top floor. Los opened the door but nobody got out. The door rested half opened on his back. The others picked a corner of the elevator and put their backs to it.

Tafari watched the topless beer bottle as it went from Los's hand to Stretch's and was being offered to his. He hesitated. Then his arm rose as if he had a dumbbell in his grip. Very sluggish and weighty. Tafari put the bottle to his lips and took a sip. It didn't take long to feel the liquid fire in his system. He felt heavy and woozy almost immediately. Tafari really didn't like the taste at all, but he drank with them anyway, just to fit in.

Ten minutes later, the empty forty-ounce beer bottle sat lonely in the corner. Tafari felt woozy in the head, trying to balance himself in the corner of the elevator.

"You a'ight, Tafari?" Lil' Headache asked.

"Yeah, I'm good," Tafari assured. It felt like everything was moving around him. Tafari took one concentrated step forward and the elevator wall seemed to take one giant leap out and crashed into him. His body crumbled and his legs gave out. Tafari rolled over on his back and an unfocused view of Lil' Headache's face hovered over him with a crooked smile zipping across his face. A thunderous laugh exploded deep from Tafari's core, as if he hadn't laughed in years. Like he was storing them and saving up laughs. That fire water found his combination and popped the box open and laughter erupted out of his mouth and detonated in the elevator. Tafari laughed so hard it hurt. He laughed so long it hurt.

They took the elevator back down to the lobby and chilled for a few minutes. The fresh air did Tafari some good. He was leaning against the wall of mailboxes tugging on the drawstrings of his hoody and counting the floor tiles when the squeaky lobby door screamed as it was yanked open. A burst of wind rushed at Tafari's face and spit dust in his right eye. It snapped him out of his hazed state of mind. He rubbed his right eye with the back of his hand while his left eye peeked at the open lobby door.

Into Tafari's view strutted a butterscotch-dipped goddess with long, jet-black, straight hair. Her eyes were cat-like and hidden behind shaded lenses. He knew she had the eyes of a cat because he had seen her many times strutting up and down the school hallways.

Regardless of who was in the school corridors or on the block, the mere presence of Malikah Shabazz would sponge all the attention. Girls would twist up their lips while goofy grins sunk in above all the guys' chins. Weren't any girls around but Tafari was certain they were somewhere, sucking their teeth and rolling their eyes at the mere thought of her.

She seemed to pose in the doorway, just long enough for the boys' half-wide crimson eyes to sample her. Her pouted lips were lip-glossy moist and her small hands were tucked into her short black leather jacket. She wore a pair of tight blue jeans that looked painted on and stood in a pair of black ankle boots.

She stopped posing and began to strut through the lobby as if it were a runway.

"Hey, Malikah," Lil' Headache cheered through a goofy grin. Malikah barely acknowledged him as she reached the elevator. Tafari tried to follow her strut but out of the corner of his eye another image flashed in front of the lobby doorway. An image that Tafari daydreamed and nightmared about and prayed he would not see again. But there he stood, blond dreads and all. And his presence still made Tafari's heart thunder in his chest.

Tafari grabbed his hoody and pulled it down to his eyes. He turned from the door and eyed the mailboxes hoping Dready didn't see his face.

"Whassup, Dready?!" Lil' Headache said.

"Yeah, mon. Respect," Dready answered back. Tafari heard them slap hands. Then he heard the elevator door drag open. Tafari didn't turn around until the elevator door slammed shut.

"I can't stand Dready," Lil' Headache revealed. "The only reason Malikah is goin' out with him is 'cause he got a little rep in the hood. I can't see Malikah dealing with him without it."

"How did he get his rep?" Tafari asked, curiously.

"Dready always had a rep as being a crazy thug. But it grew when he got into a beef with Big Mel."

"Who is Big Mel?"

"His real name is Ramel Smalls. Ring a bell?" Tafari shook his head.

"You weren't lyin' when you said you lock yaself in ya room writin' rhymes," Lil' Headache said, with a hint of sarcasm. "Big Mel was a senior at Hard Knocks. You probably saw him in school before. He used to hang out with this dude called Green-Eyes and everybody was afraid of them because they were notorious for robbing dudes of their coats, sneakers, gold chains, drugs, and pretty much anything that you had that was valuable. From what I heard, Big Mel punked Dready and took his coat. The next day in the boys locker room, Dready pulled out a knife on Big Mel and started barkin' and yellin' that he was gonna cut him if he didn't get his coat back. Dready's rep grew because nobody would dare challenge

Big Mel let alone pull a knife on him like Dready did. They said that Big Mel was scared and promised to bring the coat back the next day. Well, that next morning when I was on my way to school, there were cops crowding the front of the school. Turns out that Big Mel got caught by one of the resource officers trying to sneak a gun into the school. They said Big Mel was gonna shoot Dready for pulling the knife on him but he got bagged by five-0 and was locked up. With Big Mel in Juvie, Dready had one of the biggest reps in the school because of what he did and he kind of took over the school."

"Why do y'all call Bronx High *Hard Knocks High*?" Tafari asked.

"They call our school Hard Knocks because the school is so gangsta!" Lil' Headache declared. "If you are able to survive Hard Knocks for four years and graduate, you will have all the life lessons you would ever need."

Fareal," Los added. "If you earn a diploma from Hard Knocks, you are ready for the University of life."

"Come on, y'all," Lil' Headache urged, waving a black Sharpie in front of everyone's eyes, trying to change the subject. "Let's go up to the roof and tag our names on the wall to let everybody know that's our spot."

They took the elevator back up to the top floor. Once they got off, they entered the staircase and headed up to the top landing that led to the roof. All was quiet except for a flock of purring pigeons that normally gathered on the rooftops of the buildings when the moon popped up.

"I think somebody is on the roof," Lil' Headache said, pausing halfway up the steps. The red door to the roof was slightly opened, but they couldn't tell what was holding it open.

That's when Tafari heard a voice coming from behind the door. It was a familiar voice. Tafari nearly ran up Los's back, trying to flee from the voice.

"What's the matter witchu?" Los said, shoving Tafari back. Darkness seemed to pull the roof door open. A tan army suit jumped in front of the darkness with dirty blond dreadlocks swinging back and forth behind the twisted up face with the fiery eyes. A lit cigarette dangled between his fingers. Malikah rested her chin on his shoulder from behind to see who was making all the noise. They appeared like a two-headed creature from some second-rate movie. Dready was playing the role of the ugly twin, of course.

Tafari pulled his hood back down to his eyes and faced the wall while Dready stomped down the stairs. He felt Dready's aura next to him. Chill bumps prickled up his back. His armpits moistened.

"Whatcha doin' up here?" Dready hissed.

"My bad, dawg. We were just, um, comin' up here to the spot to tag our names on the wall," Lil' Headache stammered.

"Dis is my spot!" Dready hissed, again. "Dat's my name on de wall ova dere. It says Dready! De originoo Shatta!" Dready's feet shuffled as if he changed his stance. Tafari could feel his breath blowing on the back of his hood.

"Who dis? Him look familya," Dready asked. Tafari's heart was pounding and his gut was churning. Tafari knew Dready was talking about him but he didn't turn to face him.

"That's my homie, Tafari," Lil' Headache answered.

Suddenly, Tafari was feeling hot from the inside out and he didn't feel like himself at that point. He felt possessed, like that chick from the *Exorcist*. Maybe it was the brown fire-water he sipped out of the beer bottle. Or maybe it was the bitter memories from last week on the train cringing in front of Dready's gun, and a need, no, a *lust* to keep Dready's gun from forcing him to undress in front of his new crew like it did in front of Mahogany.

Don't know which one of them demons made him turn and face him or which one was responsible for controlling his tongue when he said, "Nah, you don't know me dawg."

"Blooood cloooooot. It's de choir bwoy!" Dready sang, his face lighting up.

"You got me mixed up with somebody else, man," Tafari said, his tongue still out of his control.

"What ya chat 'bout, mon?" Dready asked, turning to Lil' Headache. "Me just robbed dis choir bwoy 'pon de train last week. Make him walk home in him draws," Dready cackled. Lil' Headache, Stretch, and Los glared at Tafari, sizing him up as if they were questioning the new dude they just put down with them. Tafari figured they were wondering if he was the thug he presented himself to be or just some fake wannabe thug.

Tafari felt like an exposed street magician. All night long he had his audience of Lil' Headache, Stretch, and Los fooled. The thug outfit and the slick thug lyrics were a mirage and his flawed performance of being a thug was too quick for their eyes to catch. But Dready knew better. And he revealed the greatest trick Tafari ever performed.

Visions of being trapped behind his window and never being able to show his face on the other side of it flashed before Tafari's mind's eye. Whatever it was that had possession of him grew desperate. And like any good magician, Tafari needed to distract his audience so he could fool them again.

The rage was building in Tafari's chest. The fingers on his right hand curled into a tight fist. Tafari's right arm jumped from his side and his fist smashed into Dready's face. Hit Dready so hard on his right cheek, he felt the sting from his fist all the way down into his toes. Dready went down like a baseball player in the batter's box. All the way down. Down the stairs, tumbling backwards with his dreads seemingly spinning like helicopter propellers. When he rolled to a stop at the bottom platform, Tafari stomped down the stairs after him. He lifted his right Timberland boot and smashed it down on his dread locks. His Timberlands continued to stomp as if he had a stubborn roach on his head that refused to die.

Malikah stampeded down the flight of stairs and joined his crew on the platform above him and Dready. She began jumping up and down, throwing a child-like tantrum. "Get off of him! Somebody stop it! Somebody get him off of him!" Malikah screamed.

Tafari removed his right Timberland from Dready's face. Not because Malikah said so, but because the roach appeared to have died as blood appeared from under the forest of dreadlocks and trickled down the side of his face like a bead of sweat.

Dready performed magic of his own. Out of nowhere a gun appeared in his hand. The same gun he showed Tafari on the train a week ago. He aimed it at the symbol on Tafari's sweat shirt, just above his heart. Everyone backed up as Dready rose to his feet. Fire flickered in his eyes as if he was possessed by his own demons.

"Ya know who ya mess wit'!" Dready roared, spittle raining from his mouth. "Huh?! Ya know who ya blood clot mess wit'?! Ya just dead!" There was something different about Dready during their second encounter. The tough talk was the same. Even the gun was the same. But the arm that held the gun was different. It trembled. It was as if the weight of doubt crept out from behind his mind, trickled down his shoulder, and sat on his arm.

At that point, a new demon seemed to be born within Tafari. Actually, it might have been an angel. An angel of survival that took over his body and made him lunge at the gun. As Tafari grabbed at it and tried to wrestle it from Dready's grip, an explosion ripped from the gun. The purring from the pigeons gave way to a chain of flapping wings as the birds fled away from the frightening boom. Dready collapsed. A deep burgundy appeared high on his thigh and ate away at the rest of his right pant leg. Clutching his thigh, Dready howled, begged, and pleaded all at the same time, "Oh, Jah! Jah who sits high above de world in Zion, place thy blessed hands 'pon me wound and heal me, Jah! Heal me!"

The echo of Malikah's scream blared through the staircase. The demons and angel fled from Tafari as if they had been exorcised. He was left by himself, wide-eyeing the gun in his hand, surrounded by thugs with fright in their eyes.

"Hey, what's goin' on out there!" a voice called out from behind the stairwell.

"I'm callin' the cops!" another voice called out.

Lil' Headache, Stretch, and Los leapt down the whole flight of steps. Malikah remained sobbing and screaming.

"Come on, let's go!" Lil' Headache urged, grabbing Tafari's arm. Just as Tafari was about to jump down the flight of steps, he noticed Dready's gold chain and medallion by his foot. Dready didn't seem to notice that it popped off. He was too busy writhing on floor, moaning for Jah, with both hands pressed on his right leg.

Tafari didn't know why, but he scooped up the chain and stuffed it in his pocket. Tafari tucked the gun between his belt and covered it with his oversized sweatshirt. He held it in place while he skipped down the steps behind Lil' Headache.

When Tafari hit the cool night breeze, he sprinted through the streets, entered his building and went straight to the roof to change. Thoughts raced through the alleys of his mind just as fast. The face of Mahogany sat on top of each thought. He couldn't shake her from his mind. Tafari wished she was there, in the building, in the hall-way, in between the eleventh and twelfth floors.

If she were there, Tafari would have looked a lot different from the last time she saw him. Last time she saw him, he was half naked, shaking his ashy knobby knees and shrinking in front of the barrel of a gun held by the hand of a thug. But if she was there, in the hallway, she would have seen him in his new outfit. She probably wouldn't have recognized him. She definitely wouldn't have recognized the guy that wrestled that same gun out of that same hand. She would have seen the dreadlocked thug who slapped her across her face rolling around on the floor with a bullet hole in his leg, screaming and hollering because of something Tafari did to him. She would have had no reason to hide her face in her hands. Tafari couldn't wait to see her again.

Chapter 7

Tafari was alone, chillin' on the corner, leaning against the chipped, red brick walls of the deli. The streets were bare. Tafari heard the water before he saw it. Across the street, rivers of ocean water spilled from between project buildings, flooding the block and rushing toward Tafari. Before he could react, the angry water surrounded him, rising from his knees, to his waist, all the way up to his neck. Tafari sucked in a lung full of air and sealed his lips together as the water crept up to his chin. Panic set in when the water tickled his nose and Tafari remembered that he couldn't swim. He flailed his arms, splashing wildly until he noticed his gun floating by. But it looked odd. It was huge, almost like a floating device. Tafari reached out for it and the gun popped and deflated like a balloon.

"Help!"

Tafari screamed and jumped up in his bed. He glanced at the alarm clock on his night stand and realized it was time for him to be leaving for school. After dragging on his clothes, Tafari kneeled down and reached for the gun under his bed. With the Timberlands tucked in his backpack, the gun with the taped-up handle made a home out of the boot-box. He removed the lid on the box and eyed the gun while it lay snug between the sheets of wrapping tissue that normally lined the insides of sneaker boxes. Tafari pulled back the sheets and let his eyes run across the naked steel body of the thirty-eight. As his finger slid across the cold steel, chill bumps prickled up the back of his arm. As quickly as he could, Tafari tucked the gun under the sheets, slammed the lid shut, and slid it back into the darkness underneath his bed.

The plan was to remove the gun from the box and let it take new residence in his backpack, along with his rhyme book, science textbook, jeans, sweatshirt, and his Timberlands. Since the gun went off in his hand and hit Dready in the leg the night before, Tafari was worried that he might be limping through the school corridors looking for revenge. Tafari thought he would feel more at ease if he had the gun with him but his gut told him differently.

Just before Tafari headed off to school, he went to the roof and changed into his new thug uniform. Didn't matter that it was the same outfit he wore the night before. Just about all of the thugs in the projects wore the same clothes daily anyway.

Despite wearing the same outfit, he doubted anyone would notice. The wandering eyes would have a hard time not noticing the blinging gold medallion that hung from the Cuban link chain hanging from his neck. When Tafari snatched it from the ground, he thought it had popped from around Dready's neck but instead it just unhooked somehow as he fell down the stairs.

After leaving his school clothes on the roof, Tafari met up with Lil' Headache who was waiting for him in front of the building. His eyes widened at his presence. They even seemed to twinkle as if he were eyeing somebody important. Lil' Headache embraced Tafari like he hadn't seen him in twelve years rather than twelve hours ago.

"Whassup, Tafari! What's good?!" Lil' Headache cheered.

"Chillin'. Hey, you going to school today?" Tafari asked, noticing Lil' Headache was wearing a backpack.

"Yeah, you sound shocked."

"That's because I am. You hardly ever come to school."

"Before I had no reason to. Unless I wanted to get harassed by Dready and his boys. But now that you are down with our crew, it's all good. The way you handled him last night, I doubt we will ever hear from Dready again."

"Why don't you think we'll hear from him again?"

"I heard he went back to Jamaica," Lil' Headache said. Tafari wanted to be relieved, but Lil' Headache said he *heard.* When someone in the projects said they *heard,* it usually meant it was just a rumor or they just made it up. Tafari never understood why so many people in the projects got a kick out of making stuff up. Just lying for no good reason.

A short kid wearing a tilted Yankee hat, who couldn't have been older than twelve, was staring at Tafari a few feet away. Like Lil' Headache, he too had that star-struck gaze in his eyes. Unlike Lil' Headache, he hesitated to approach Tafari. His eyes danced and soaked in Tafari's presence as if he were a ghetto celebrity. Made Tafari feel a little uneasy. Probably the way most celebrities felt when out in public knowing eyes were all over them.

"Whassup, Tafari?!" said the kid in the Yankee hat, finally finding the nerve to approached him.

"Whassup, bruh?!" Tafari said, wondering how the kid even knew him.

"I heard you were chasing Dready through the staircase last night and popped him four times."

"What?" Tafari responded, dumbfounded.

"Yeah, and I heard he was crying and begging you for his life."

"Where did you hear that?"

"It's all over the streets, man." Tafari and the boy slapped hands and he bopped off smiling as if he had given him an autograph. Tafari realized that it didn't take long for the real-life hood movie that jumped off between the eleventh and twelfth floors starring Tafari and Dready just the night before had already circulated through the projects like a bootleg DVD. The original script had been edited. Some scenes were deleted and new ones were added. Somehow the ending had been deleted so people started to draw their own dramatic conclusions.

"See, your name is all over the streets. I went back outside last night and all everybody was talking about was you."

"Me?"

"Yup. They were sayin' some gangsta dude named Tafari bucked Dready in the leg and sent him back to Jamaica."

"You sure he went back to Jamaica, or are they just making it up?"

"Nah, he really is in Jamaica. His girl Malikah told my home girl Kesha that his mom got scared and was sending him back to Jamaica to live with is grandmother before he got killed out in these streets. I heard he went straight from the hospital to the airport last night. After what you did to him, he couldn't show his face around here no more anyway. Now everybody knows he was just frontin'. I mean all he really did was wave a knife at Big Mel. Anybody could do that. Everyone doesn't have the heart to pull the trigger like you did."

I actually never had the heart to pull the trigger myself, Tafari thought. *It just kind of went off in my hand. But I don't plan on sharing that part of the script with Lil' Headache or anybody else in the projects. I'll just keep that little secret between me and the heart I never had.*

Relief embraced Tafari like a comforter upon the realization that Dready was thousands of miles away on an island. The chain around Tafari's neck and those edited stories put him on his own island in the projects. Tafari stood alone amongst the young thugs. Similar to being in his window all those years looking down on the world, but this time, all the eyes were looking up at him.

Tafari and Lil' Headache entered the thick, steel front doors of Bronx High just before the tardy bell. He was just in time for his Hamlet exam, which he wasn't ready for. Tafari was pulling a strong B in Language Arts but that grade was soon to be in serious jeopardy. That exam could have easily been written in French or German because it looked foreign to him. Over the past few weeks, his mind was too preoccupied to study for some stupid Hamlet exam. He had real life exams that he had to pass every day. Exams with questions like, how long can he continue to dodge Mahogany's searching eyes in the cluttered halls of Bronx High and her phone calls at home and on his cell? How many times can he skip Bible study and the teen rap session before Mom finds out? When were his new homies, Lil' Headache, Stretch, and Los, going to figure out that he was really a church-going homebody and not the street thug that he was pretending to be? Thus far, he was passing his life exam with flying colors. Couldn't say the same about the Hamlet exam, though.

After first period, Tafari rushed down to the first floor because Mahogany had some kind of dance or jazz class which was right next to the gym. Tafari no longer wanted to avoid Mahogany; he went looking for her. He wanted to tell her the good news. He wanted to tell her what he did to Dready. But instead of running into her, he ran into Lil' Headache, Stretch, and Los hanging out by the entrance of the boys locker room. "Over here homie," Los called out, the first one to spot Tafari. "We were just talking about you."

"Good things, I hope," Tafari replied.

"It's all good, bruh." They slapped hands and gave each other a half hug. Tafari began to say something to Los but his words trailed off. The end of his sentence was incomprehensible. Tafari had no idea what he said or how he ended that sentence but he *did* know what he saw. Malikah rounded the corner with a textbook in her hand. Tafari always got brain freeze when he saw Malikah. That was the first time he saw her since she was jumping up and down screaming at the sight of Dready's blood the night before.

Malikah's lips inched apart with each ankle-boot step in his direction, revealing her straight whites, almost tooth by tooth. By the time she got up on Tafari, her straight whites were gleaming. Tafari didn't offer a smile back, though. Wanted to. But he bit down on his bottom lip to keep his teeth from spilling out of his mouth. *Why was Dready's girl smiling at me?* Tafari wondered. *Especially after what I did to her boyfriend.* Confusion wrinkled his brows as he analyzed her smile looking for some type of sinister motive behind it. The motive wasn't obvious, so he tried his best to seal his lips tight and keep his teeth hidden because no girl that looked as good as Malikah ever offered him a smile like that.

So much for containing his excitement. As Malikah strutted passed him, her free hand reached out and gently squeezed Tafari's. She glanced back at Tafari and seductively bit into her bottom lip before she disappeared around the corner. Tafari was a bundle of confused energy. He wanted to skip down the hall and chase after her, but Los put a hand on Tafari's shoulder.

"Did Malikah just grab ya hand, yo?" Los asked, his voice soaked with excitement.

"Yeah, you saw that?!"

"I think she wants to get witchu," Lil' Headache said, eyes full of awe. "I been wantin' to get with her for a while now and she ain't never look at me like she just looked atchu. So whatchu gonna do?" Tafari wasn't sure what to do. A voice whispered deep from the well of his brain: *But what about Mahogany? I really like her, but she did turn her back on me when I needed her most,* the voice reasoned. *I mean, if she was really down for me and really loved me, she wouldn't have left me on the train platform after I was humiliated. A real girl who was down for her man would have at least walked me home and vowed to help me get revenge.*

Cut the BS, Tafari, another voice cut in. *She was just as scared as you were. What was she supposed to do? You are the one that knows what's real in the streets, right? You said you were going to protect her, right?* Tafari's feelings were a rope and the two voices engaged in a taxing game of tug of war, pulling them in different directions.

Tafari sat in the middle of World Geography class with his head heavy with thoughts. Laughter, loud incoherent chatter, and random yelps surrounded Tafari from all sides of the noisy classroom. Mrs. Yeager was steady scribbling away on the board and hardly anyone noticed. Tafari always wondered why she wasted her time when only the three nerdy girls who sat up front paid any attention to her. Everyone else chatted with neighbors, threw paper balls across the room, or just roamed around aimlessly.

"Yo, Tafari," a student called out from the front of the class. Tafari lifted his head from his arms and locked eyes with the student. "Headache is at the door looking for you," the student said. Tafari raised his hand, but as usual Mrs. Yeager had her back to the class and her face to the board. Tafari walked to the front of the class and saw Lil' Headache's face pressed on the glass of the front door. "Mrs. Yeager, I'm going to the restroom," Tafari announced. Mrs. Yeager just looked at him without saying a word. He snatched the plastic restroom pass that hung from a hook by the door and walked out.

"I just saw Malikah," Lil' Headache said. "She told me to tell you to meet her by the girls' restroom."

"Did she say why?"

"Nah, she just told me to tell you to come now. But I wouldn't go if I were you," Lil' Headache warned.

"Why?"

"You just shot her man. It could be a set up."

"Didn't you say he's in Jamaica now?"

"Yeah, that's what I heard. But still, I wouldn't trust her."

"If you were me, would you go?" Tafari asked.

"Hell yeah!" Lil' Headache cheered. He and Tafari laughed and slapped hands. "She looks too good for you not to at least find out what she wants," Lil' Headache reasoned.

Tafari followed Lil' Headache down the hall until he stopped and pointed at the door of the girls' restroom. Tafari looked both ways, making sure the halls were clear of security. He tapped on the door with his knuckles. Malikah opened it immediately as if she was standing on the other side of the door waiting on him.

Tafari hesitated. He had never stepped foot in the girls' restroom before. Even though he wanted to on many occasions. Many times he would be walking by the restroom as a girl was opening the door going in or coming out and his eyes would strain, trying to take in as much as they could before the door would close shut.

But that time, he was being invited in. But still, he hesitated. He was afraid there might be boys hiding behind the restroom door instead of girls. Dready and his boys, that is. But with the project goddess standing in the doorway with her bow-legged stance and a cherubic smile Tafari could hesitate no more. She rarely smiled at anyone from the projects let alone looked at them. Usually saved her smiles and cat-like stares for thugs that carried big guns and held even bigger reputations.

Upon his entrance, the first thing Tafari noticed were the pink walls. He also noticed there were more stalls in the girls' restroom and no urinals. After satisfying his curiosity of the girls' restroom, and realizing they were the only two in between the pink walls, Tafari turned his curious eyes to Malikah. Her eyes were all over him. They danced across his face, dipped down to his Timberlands and bounced back up to his eyes. Her eyes had a look in them. The same look Mahogany had in her eyes on the train that night just before Dready and Donovan appeared and messed everything up. That look spoke to Tafari and told him that Mahogany wanted him. Malikah had the same look, but it was something strange about it. *Where did that look come from and why was it in her eyes?* Tafari knew where Mahogany's came from. They knew each other for years. To know him was to love him was what Tafari always said. But Malikah didn't know him. *So where did that look come from?*

Malikah approached Tafari, almost in slow motion. Felt unreal, like a dream.

"Whassup, boo?" Malikah said, gnawing on her bottom lip, seductively.

"Nothin'. Whassup witchu?" Tafari asked, his heart pounding.

"So, what's good wit' me and you?"

"Whatchu mean?"

"I'm tryna get witchu. So what's up?"

"I don't know. What's good witchu and Dready?"

"Dready? Please! I don't mess with him no more."

"Why not?"

"I thought he was real, but he showed his skirt when you made him cry and run back to Jamaica. I need me a real *man*, like you." *Can I really trust her?* Tafari thought. *Can I really believe her?*

"You don't believe me, do you?" Malikah asked, as if she was eaves dropping on Tafari's internal conversation. Tafari shrugged. "What do I have to do to prove it to you?" Malikah asked, her cat eyes hypnotizing Tafari. Tafari knew what he wanted to say, but he couldn't fix his mouth to say what his mind was suggesting. He realized immediately that he didn't have to. Malikah was still listening in. Her beautiful face leaned towards his. Malikah's moist lips pressed on his and they kissed slowly. Suddenly, the bathroom door squeaked open. Tafari's heart jumped. The sound of the door meant someone was entering. Tafari was afraid that someone was going to be

Dready and his boys. Tafari pulled away from Malikah and braced for another beat down.

To his relief, if it's possible to be relieved that he was about to get caught in the girls' restroom, a freckled face girl appeared before them. The moment froze. They all stared at each other. Freckle Face's mouth dropped and her eyes widened at the sight of Tafari.

"Well?" Malikah yelled at the girl. "Why are you still standin' there?! Get the hell outta here!" Freckle Face cowered and raced out of the bathroom as if she were being chased. Malikah turned back to Tafari, the cherubic smile returning to her lips.

"So, do you believe me now?" Malikah asked, her voice soft.

"Yeah, I believe you."

"So, do you gotta girlfriend?"

"Um . . . kind of."

"What do you mean, kind of?" Malikah chuckled. "Either you do or you don't."

"Well, I did. But we haven't spoken for a week."

"So, y'all had a fight?"

"Not really a fight. Just a disagreement."

"So, you're not sure if ya'll are still going out?"

"I guess we still are," Tafari shrugged.

"It don't matter. I know she don't look as good as me," Malikah said, confidently, easing into a pose. The same pose she probably struck a million times when taking her own picture with her camera phone. Tafari's eyes hungrily devoured every inch of her pose. He couldn't believe someone as beautiful as Malikah wanted to get with him. Malikah strutted toward Tafari and gently put his hand in hers. "So, you gonna get wit' me or what?" A gang of butterflies ambushed Tafari's stomach. He felt hot from the inside out like that night when he was sipping on that fire water. And just like that infamous night, he didn't feel like he was in control of himself. It was as if someone was the ventriloquist to his actions and words. And Tafari had an idea that Malikah was well schooled at making guys say what she wanted.

"Um . . . yeah," Tafari stammered, through a goofy grin.

"Okay. So, now I'm ya girl." Malikah wrapped her arms around Tafari. His legs were wet noodles and what started as a hug turned into Malikah holding Tafari up. It wasn't until Tafari went to math class and was out of the reach of Malikah's spell that he realized what he had done. Just like in his previous class, his head was heavy. But more than just his head, his heart was heavy.

Chapter 8

It wasn't really Tafari that sat in the back on them wooden bench seats in between two ladies with Bibles on their laps, waving fans at the beads of sweat that moistened their pudgy faces. It was just a shell of Tafari. Instead of being in the cramped oven that passed for a church, Tafari's mind and spirit was on the corner in front of Papi's Deli, chillin' in between Lil' Headache, Stretch, and Los.

It was only an occasional outburst by one of the older ladies sitting on either side of Tafari, popping out their seats like someone just lit their butts on fire, shouting and stomping in place, that would snatch him from the corner and toss him back into his shell of a body.

After a half hour, all of the teens were dismissed downstairs for the youth service. Rows of metal folding chairs were set up in the cramped basement of the church. Tafari took a seat toward the back as the chairs were filling up quickly. Preston Kyle Williams, who everyone called PK, was just appointed the Youth Pastor of the church. He stood in front of the teens praising the Lord and thanking everyone for coming out. While PK spoke, Tafari noticed Mahogany, who sat a few rows ahead of him, turning in her seat every minute to sneak peeks at him. That was the first time Tafari saw her since that infamous night on the train.

Mahogany's face looked different in the church. The expression on her face, that is. It wasn't the same expression she wore on the train that night after Dready walked out with Tafari's clothes bunched in his arms. The same expression Tafari was trying hard to avoid while pretending to be sick so he could stay home from church and had him avoiding the familiar routes that he and she traveled to and from classes together.

"Before we wrap up, I want to recognize the F.O.G of the month," PK announced. "This brother helps out behind the scenes, volunteers his time, and is a great mentor to our youth. He is a true follower of God. I present this award to Tafari King." Applause filled the church basement as a stunned Tafari made his way to the front to accept the cardstock award. After accepting his award, everyone joined hands in prayer before being dismissed for the day.

"I don't know if I deserve this award," Tafari admitted to PK after pulling him aside.

"Of course you do," PK assured. "You volunteer your time by coming early on Sundays to help set up and clean—"

"I think you might wanna give this award to my mom." Tafari shrugged. "She kind of forces me to come early and help out."

"It's more than just the volunteering. You've been a great mentor to some of the youth here as well. There are some teens here that really admire you and look to you as a mentor."

"Like who?"

"The twins. They speak very highly of you and so does their mom. Plus, I admire you, too."

"You?" Tafari asked, shock in his voice. "How could you admire me when you were hand picked by the Pastor to serve as the Youth Pastor? We're supposed to admire you."

"I'm in no position to be admired," PK stated.

"Why not?"

"I'm not spiritually equipped to lead my fellow teens anywhere," PK said. "I'm just not ready yet."

"You seem ready to me," Tafari said. "Every Sunday you're—"

"I wear a mask on Sundays," PK revealed. "It's a show. I do what I gotta do because everyone expects me to do it. A lotta people are counting on me. What you see on Sundays is not the real me. Or at least, it's not the only me."

"What do you mean, not the only you?"

"You know how it is trying to be a teen nowadays. The girls . . . trying to fit in with the guys . . . it's a lotta temptations and pressure out there. That's why I admire you. Me and you are the same age, and yet, somehow you managed to avoid the traps that I'm struggling with." *Little does he know,* Tafari thought. At that point, the adults were ascending down stairs, led by the Pastor who stopped at the entrance and summoned PK. Tafari spotted Mahogany a moment ago but lost her eyes in the crowd of bodies. Soon, another pair of eyes, beaming like high beams, was bearing down on Tafari. Tafari recognized that those eyes belonged to the boy whose bike he stole. Quickly, Tafari went for his backpack and darted between the traffic of bodies and escaped the boy's oncoming, high-beaming eyes. Tafari ran into his mom who was waiting at the top of the steps.

"There's my son. I've been looking for you," Mom said, wrapping her arms around Tafari. "I'm so proud of you son. I heard about your award. Let me see it." Just as Tafari handed his award to Mom, Ms. Green approached from behind.

"Hey, Sister King? Wonderful service today, huh?"

"Amen."

"Listen, I just wanted to tell you how wonderful your son is. It's always been a struggle to get Noel and Leon ready for church on Sunday mornings. But lately, they've been so excited to come to church that they get up before

I do and are dressed and ready to go. All because they can't wait to see Tafari. They really look up to him."

"Thank you for the kind words. I can't tell you enough how proud I am of Tafari. He never gives me any problems, he stays out of trouble, and he has shown to be an excellent role model for your sons and all of the teens here. I couldn't ask for a better son." Mom kissed Tafari on the forehead. Her words beat at Tafari's conscience as he thought about the road he'd been traveling. A road Mom knew nothing about. One of guns, lies, stolen bikes, thugs, and alcohol. "Come with me back downstairs and eat because I ain't cooking when we get home," Mom declared.

"No thanks," Tafari began, nervously checking over his shoulder in search of the high beams. "You know I don't like nasty church food."

"Boy, hush up. Ain't nothing wrong with the food here."

"Who cooked it?"

"Sister Henrietta did most of the cooking at home. She's setting up in the kitchen downstairs."

"She got over a dozen cats in her house," Tafari complained. "I ain't eating anything she cooked in that litter box she calls a home."

"Boy, you watch your mouth. That's an adult you are talking about. Sister Henrietta is a good woman. She cooks most of the food all by herself and she doesn't ask for a dime. Now close your mouth and be thankful that you have something to eat. There are plenty of starving kids in this world that don't know where their next meal is coming from." *If them starving kids knew their next meal was being made in Sister Henrietta's house with bunch of cat sous chefs, I'm sure they'd rather starve,* Tafari thought.

"Well, Mom, can't you let your role model of a son skip out on dinner at the church just this one time? Please."

"Tafari, I done told you I ain't cooking tonight."

"I know, I know. I'll just eat some Lucky Charms or I'll make a turkey and cheese sandwich or something."

"Alright. You make sure you go straight home, honey."

"I will." Tafari merged with the flow of bodies that exited the church. As Tafari made his way through the crowd of bodies, he reconnected with the eyes that were sneaking peeks at him in church. That time, the eyes weren't sneaking peeks at him; it was an obvious peek. A long peek.

The expression on Mahogany's face changed once it hit the sun. Daylight seemed to make her expression sag, hound-dog-like. She tucked her chin in her neck and her head slumped, making her eyes look up at Tafari as if he was the master to her hound-dog expression. This expression told Tafari, no, barked at him, loudly, that she'd been missing him. Tafari thought he heard the expression apologize to him. Tafari's lips wrinkled into a smirk, his way of accepting her apology. Then the wrinkle in his lips straightened out like a crease and he mimicked her hound-dog expression and apologized back. Her teeth grew from under her lips until her lips disappeared and her expression now was all bright wide eyes and teeth and gums in front of him. That expression seemed to be telling Tafari what happened two weeks ago on the train was forgotten.

Mahogany approached Tafari with arms spread like wings and wrapped them around him until they were full of each other. She pulled away and jabbed moisture from the corner of her right eye with her index finger. "Your mom will kill you if she finds out that you are here," Tafari said.

"I know, I know," Mahogany responded. "But I really wanted to see you."

Tafari grabbed her hand and led her away from the church, pulling her into the small alley that separated the church from C Town.

"They better hurry up," Tafari said, looking back at the church.

"Who better hurry up?" Mahogany asked.

"Them," Tafari answered, pointing at the twins who were racing toward the alley.

"Okay, can we see it now?" Leon asked, half out of breath. Tafari looked around the corner one last time to make sure they weren't being followed. He dipped his hand into his backpack and pulled out the gun. Beams of light glistened off of the barrel, which Tafari assumed was the sun, but it could have been the twins' eyes which lit up at the sight of the thirty-eight.

"Can I hold it?" Noel asked, excitedly, reaching for the gun.

"Hurry up," Tafari said, quickly.

"Bah! Bah! Bah! Bah! Take that! Take that!" Noel grunted, pretending to shoot the gun while squeezing the handle with two hands.

"Alright," Tafari chuckled. "That's enough." Tafari removed the gun from Noel's hand.

"Hey, I didn't get a chance to hold it!" Leon whined.

"Maybe next time. Remember, don't say nothin' to ya mom."

"Come on, dawg. You know we ain't gon' say nothin' to Ma-Dukes," Noel assured.

"Word up," Leon added, he and his brother both trying to sound like the thugs that hang below their window. "We ain't snitches." The twins headed back to the church.

"Tafari, where did you get that gun?" Mahogany gasped.

"This gun don't look familiar to you?"

"No. Should it?"

"Yeah, it should." Tafari kneeled down and removed his jeans, Timberlands and sweatshirt from his backpack and put the gun and his Follower of God award back in.

"What are you doing?" Mahogany asked.

"Changing," Tafari said, kicking off his scuffed-up shoes and pulling his jeans over his dress pants.

"Why?"

"I *have* to."

"For what? You never changed before."

"That's because *before* I was a punk," Tafari said, pulling his hooded sweatshirt over his white shirt.

"What are you talking about?"

"It's true. And you know it's true. You were there, 'member?"

"Yeah, but Tafari, I been wanting to tell you—"

"Before, those thugs looked at me as someone to pick on and someone to rob and make fun of. But when I started changin', things started changin' for me. Now I'm the *man*," Tafari declared, thumping his chest with a closed fist.

"What do you mean, you're the man?" Mahogany asked.

"Remember that night on the train—" Memories of that night barged into Tafari's mind and interrupted his words. Mahogany jumped in and offered her own words. Words that she had probably been saving up, trying to give to Tafari since that night, but he had been avoiding her. She took a deep breath before giving them to Tafari.

"Tafari, listen, I've been wanting to tell you this for a while now," Mahogany said, her words were quick as if she couldn't hold it in any longer. "What happened on the train that night was humiliating, it was degrading, it was embarrassing, and I have to admit, that night, I was a little mad at you. No, I'm lying; I was a lot mad at you. I mean, I thought you could have stood up to them a little more. Stood up for *me*. But you didn't. You just—"

"Acted like a punk!"

"Well, I wouldn't go that far, but you just stood there and watched them eat my food and then, when he slapped me, and you didn't do anything, I was hurt and I was ashamed. But then, when I got home, the more I thought about it, I was less mad at you and madder at the situation. I realized there wasn't anything you could really do about it."

"There was a lot I could have done about it," Tafari disagreed. "In fact, I already did something about it. I only wish you could have been there to see it. "

"What do you mean?"

"I got back at Dready."

"Dready? Who is that?"

"The dreadlocked dude that pulled a gun on me on the train."

"How did you get back at him?"

"I took his gun from him and popped him in his leg with his own gun," Tafari said, proudly. "I even took his chain." Tafari pulled the medallion out from under his shirt. Horrified disbelief obscured Mahogany's face. She stood in silence for a minute, sizing up the boy in front of her. From his boots, to his pants, and hooded sweatshirt. To the medallion that hung from the gold chain around his neck, to the backpack on his back with the gun in it. The expression on her face let Tafari know that she didn't recognize him. Slowly, the grimace on her face loosened up and the light that Mahogany usually carried in her eyes lit up again. Before long, it appeared as if the sun had come down and set on her face. That expression shouted to Tafari that it liked what it was seeing.

While Tafari continued to tell Mahogany how he punked Dready, those high beams that he avoided in the church were now on the sidewalk and had tracked down Tafari on the side of the church.

"Hey, Josiah. What's the matter?" Mahogany asked, as Josiah approached.

"This dude took my bike!" Josiah shouted.

"Tafari, is this true?" Before Tafari could answer, Josiah was in his face. "I want my bike back!"

"You need to get outta my face!" Tafari warned, taking a slight step backward.

"The only reason you were able to take my bike is because you had ya boys with you. You ain't so bad without ya boys, huh?" Josiah gave Tafari a light shove.

"Put your hands on me again and see what happens!" Tafari threatened.

"Whatchu gon' do about it?" Josiah grunted, shoving Tafari again. "I can't believe they gave you the F.O.G award when you out here in the streets terrorizing innocent people. I'm gonna tell everybody in the church that you are a fraud!" Tafari reacted quicker than he could form a reasonable thought. His hand was in and out of his backpack in a flash. The thirty-eight was in his grip and the barrel was in Josiah's stomach.

"Now, what were you sayin'?" Tafari said, with a sinister tone in his voice. Josiah's eyes widened at the sight of the steel aiming at his navel. "Oh my God!" Josiah shrieked. His body jerked away from the gun. Clumsily, he stumbled into the wall of the church, ping-ponged into Mahogany, and fell to the ground, genuflecting before the gun. "I-I'm sorry! P-p-please don't kill me!"

"Now, look at who ain't so bad now," Tafari said, a sinister grin on his lips to match his tone.

"Tafari!" Mahogany yelped, horror back in her eyes.

"You can k-keep the bike. Just don't, don't shoot me. Pleeeeaaaase!" Josiah pleaded, hands together in prayer.

"Let me tell you somethin'. Don't you ever step to me like that again," Tafari warned, his bulging eyes joining in with his twisted smirk and voice to complete the sinister facial package. "And you better not snitch on me either. If you do, next time, I'm gon' use this gun. You must not know about me on these streets. You betta ask somebody." Tears were streaming down Josiah's face. He tried to speak but only grunts and groans managed to escape between his sobs. "Now, get outta here!" Tafari barked. Josiah jumped up and stumbled out of the alley way. The taste of power was sweet. Tafari's ego began to lust for more to eat.

Quickly, Tafari shoved the gun back into his backpack. Mahogany took a step back, away from Tafari.

"What's the matter witchu?" Tafari asked.

"Me? What's the matter with you?" Mahogany shot back. "As a matter of fact, who are you? I can't believe you just pulled a gun on Josiah on the side of a church. I can't believe you brought that gun into the church in the first place. I don't even recognize you anymore. It was just a few weeks ago when we sat on the train and talked about how we had so much in common. Now, I can't help but notice all the differences."

"So whatchu sayin'?"

"I'm just sayin' it's a lot to take in right now."

"So, are you sayin' you wanna break up with me?"

"No, I'm not saying that. I'm just saying I need time to think."

"You need time to think about us, right?"

"Well, it's almost like I have a new boyfriend. The person standing in front of me isn't the boy I fell in love with. It's like, I have to get to know the new you and learn to love you all over again."

"Do you think you can do that? Do you think you can accept the new me?"

"Is this the permanent you?"

"Whatchu see is whatchu get. I ain't goin' back to the old me. I didn't enjoy gettin' jumped and robbed and having guns pulled out on me. If somebody's gotta pull out the guns and do the robbin' then I rather do that than be somebody's victim." Tafari noticed tears welling up in Mahogany's eyes. Then it got quiet. So quiet that Tafari swore he heard Mahogany's heart breaking.

"I gotta go," Mahogany mentioned, checking her watch. "I think I just need to sleep on this. Meet me before school tomorrow so we can walk to school and talk, okay?"

"Alright," Tafari said, barely above a whisper, not bothering to hide his disappointment.

Chapter 9

The next morning, Tafari was up and ready for school by five, in and out of the shower by five after five and was dressed five minutes after that. Tafari spent the remaining two and a half hours in and out of the bathroom, pacing the hall and picking up things all over the apartment that he never noticed before. He just felt them in his hands for a few seconds then put them back down. Anything to busy his fidgety fingers.

Tafari had never been so awake before going to school in his life. Usually, Mom had to drag him out of the bed minutes before he was supposed to leave for school. He rarely bothered to shower when he woke up so he would just drag his clothes on and drag through the apartment until he dragged himself through the front door and on to school.

But that morning, before school was different. For the first time, he was going to meet a girl before school. He wasn't sure what to expect when they met which was why he was so antsy.

By the time he reached the front of the building, a line of students were already emerging from the lobby doors. Tafari took a seat on the bench in front of the building, his eyes searching eagerly through the hoard of students for her face. Finally, the girl he had been looking for appeared.

"Hey, Boo," Malikah said, softly. She stepped into Tafari's body and snuggled up in his arms. Malikah called Tafari on the phone the night before and asked him to walk her to school. Tafari's thoughts of both Malikah and Mahogany were playing tug of war in his mind. On one end of the rope was Mahogany, a girl he grew up with and cared for but wasn't sure how she felt about him anymore. On the other end of the rope was Malikah, the baddest girl in the projects who said she cared about him but he still had his suspicions. The way Mahogany was acting and speaking on the side of the church weighed heavy on Tafari's brain and caused her to fall behind in the game. Add Malikah's stunning beauty and reputation as the projects' goddess and she was able to win, easily.

"Thanks for picking me up, Boo," Malikah said, through an ear-to-ear smile.

"Anything for you," Tafari stated. As they strolled toward Bronx High, Malikah's hand crawled into Tafari's. Her hand tugged and gently pulled on Tafari's like a brake, making him slow down his strut, causing them to cruise down the path to school. Students were passing them on the left side, their eyes, about as bright as a cop's spotlight, were all over the new couple. Malikah's smile widened under the heat of the eyes.

"I'm so glad we're together," Malikah said.

"Me too," Tafari smiled.

"We're like the Beyoncé and Jay-Z of the school."

"Why do you say that?"

"Look at how everyone is sweatin' us." Tafari glanced around at all of the students walking along side of them. As usual, the guys were straining their necks and eyes to get a glimpse of Malikah. But what wasn't usual were the girls grinning at him as they walked by. He wasn't sure if it was because of his new rep, his new girl, or both. Either way, Tafari loved the attention.

"Even the *couples* are staring at us. I guess we are the king and queen of Bronx High," Tafari admitted. In her glee, Malikah squeezed Tafari's hand. "Ouch! You scratched me with your ring," Tafari said, adjusting her hand in his.

"Sorry 'bout that, Boo."

"That's a nice ring. Where did you get it?"

"Dready bought it for me." Tafari seethed in silence, glaring at the nugget ring. Even though Tafari had taken Dready's place in the streets, took his chain and his girl, his mark was still left behind on her ring finger. "Why are you still wearing Dready's ring?" Tafari asked.

"This ain't Dready's ring. He gave it to me so it's *my* ring."

"Well, I don't like you wearing it."

"Why?"

"Because . . . you and Dready ain't together anymore, right?"

"Of course not. I'm witchu."

"Alright then. So take off the ring."

"You still ain't tell me why you don't like me wearing it."

"That ring is like a constant reminder of your relationship with him. It's like y'all still have some type of connection, and I don't like it."

"Trust me, I don't think about him when I look at this ring. He's the furthest thing from my mind. It's all about you, Boo." Malikah hooked her arm underneath Tafari's arm.

"If it's all about me, then take off the ring."

"If you get me a bigger ring, I'll take it off." *Bigger ring?* Tafari thought. *I would have to save my allowance for months.* Either way, Tafari was determined to cut off the connection between Dready and Malikah.

Tafari walked Malikah to class, and then met up with Lil' Headache, Stretch, and Los by the gym between first and second period. "Yo, I'm starvin' already," Tafari mentioned, after giving dap to his homies. "I can't wait for lunch."

"Lucky for you, here comes Biz," Lil' Headache responded, pointing toward the crowd. Emerging from the crowd was a short, brown-skinned kid with an oversized knapsack. "Whassup, Biz?" Lil' Headache called out. "Whatchu sellin' today?"

"If you want it, I got it. If I ain't got it, I'll get it. So get it while the gettin's good." Biz removed his knapsack from his back, kneeled down and tugged on the zipper. Stretch was the first to place his order. "Yo, lemme get a Snicker bar."

"One dollar!" Biz called back to Stretch. Biz unzipped his knapsack, allowing Tafari and his crew a glimpse inside. It looked as if Biz had aisle two of Papi's Deli in his knapsack. Dozens of chocolate bars, gums, taffies, cupcakes, and potato chips. "Ohhh, you got Tasty Kakes?" Tafari sang. "Lemme get two packs of the Butterscotch Krimpetts." After Biz completed Lil' Headache's and Los's orders and collected his money, he zipped up his bag and thanked his customers for their services.

"Yo, how did you get the name Biz?" Tafari asked.

"When I first learned to walk, I used to get into everything," Biz explained. "I was real busy. Biz is short for busy. Now that I'm older, Biz is short for businessman, know what 'm sayin'?"

"Yeah, I know whatchu sayin'," Tafari laughed. Biz and Tafari gave each other dap and a half hug. Just over Biz's shoulder, Tafari saw a familiar face tucked in the crowd of approaching students. It was Donovan. A wholesome light-skinned girl with a shoulder-length weave was walking on one side of him and a brown-skinned, short dude was on the other side, bopping with a pair of headphones on his ears.

Tafari and Donovan's eyes met. Tafari wasn't sure how to react. Memories of what happened last time their eyes met danced across Tafari's mind and almost made his eyes back down. Until he realized Donovan's eyes were different. They weren't the same eyes that stared him down on the train. Those eyes looked tamed, just like Tafari's eyes on the train. Donovan's eyes had fear in them, for some reason. Then they hesitated and rolled away from Tafari's and looked to the floor. *He must have heard that I sent his friend back to Jamaica with a hole in his leg*, Tafari thought.

All of a sudden, it was like they traded eyes. Donovan had Tafari's from the train and Tafari had his. With new eyes, new confidence, and Lil' Headache, Stretch, and Los at his back, Tafari stepped into Donovan's path.

"Whassup, homie?!" Tafari called out. Donovan looked startled. His eyes were scrambling across Tafari's face, studying his demeanor, trying to figure out his motives, if any. Tafari could see him scrambling for words to respond. Donovan didn't find any so he just nodded at Tafari. Tafari looked over at the girl's round face and noticed the thick gold chain that choked her neck.

"I like ya girl's chain, homie," Tafari said.

"Um, thanks." Donovan hesitated. "I gotta get to my class." He grabbed his girl by her hand and attempted to walk around Tafari, but he cut him off again. "Lemme see that chain, man!" Tafari demanded, pointing at the girl's neck. "I'm thinkin' 'bout gettin' a chain just like that for my girl. I just wanna see how big it is." Donovan slipped his index finger under the chain and lifted it from her black shirt to give Tafari a better look.

"You know what I mean!" Tafari snapped. "Lemme hold the chain, man! I ain't goin' nowhere!"

His eyes, like Tafari's on the train, pleaded with him not to do what he was about to do. Pleaded with Tafari not to involve his girl as Tafari's eyes did, begging him to leave Mahogany alone. But Donovan's remorseless, distant eyes weren't trying to see Tafari's pleas. *Donovan seemed to enjoy eating Mahogany's food while staring all up in my helpless eyes while on the train,* Tafari thought. *The helplessness seemed to add wood to the fire that burned in his eyes. Getting robbed in front of Mahogany was humiliating enough, but to have her get robbed of her food and slapped while I stood by and did nothing made me feel like less of a man. And Donovan saw all of that in my eyes. He was literally eating it up—rice, peas, jerk-chicken, my humiliation, the whole aluminum pan.*

But in the school corridor, Donovan was looking through Tafari's eyes from the train and into the eyes Tafari borrowed from him. He could see that Tafari's eyes were determined to return the favor.

Donovan studied the gold medallion that hung from Tafari's neck and they widened with more fear. Then he noticed Lil' Headache, Stretch, and Los at his side.

Donovan threw his arms around his girl's neck and began unhooking the chain.

"What are you doin'?" She snapped, shoving at Donovan. "I ain't givin' him my chain!"

"Chill! Chill! I'ma get it back! He just wants to see it for a minute. Calm down!" She folded her arms and pouted her lips as he removed the chain from her neck and handed it to Tafari.

Tafari stuffed the chain in his pocket and stepped away from Donovan. Tafari, Lil' Headache, Stretch, and Los joked and laughed with each other while Donovan and his girl stood and watched. It was like he wasn't even there. Like it never happened.

"I gotta get to class. Can . . . can I get the chain back?"

"You still here? Yo, I'ma hold on to the chain for a little while." Tafari turned his back to him. A puzzle formed on his girl's face. She saw that he was bigger than Tafari, but what she didn't see was that Tafari's reputation was bigger than Donovan's. "I ain't leavin' without my chain!" she barked. Donovan grabbed her by the arm and yanked her to his side. "I'm gonna get it back. Relax," he promised.

"Faget that! It's my chain and I want it back, now! Ain'tchu gonna do somethin'?!"

"I said I'll get it later! C'mon, let's just go!" Despite his words, his eyes seemed to tell her it was nothing he could do. She seemed to be having trouble understanding his eyes. Tafari imagined she had never seen those eyes on him before but Tafari would have bet she'd seen those eyes on many of her man's robbery victims. He was notorious for robbing people in the projects. Those eyes were probably what attracted her ghetto-fabulous butt to him in the first place, but now, those eyes belonged to Tafari.

In an instant, Tafari's rep grew bigger. Students who were hanging around looked at Tafari with strange admiration, making him feel like he was ten feet tall in the hall. The short kid was still standing there even after Donovan and his girl left. Lil' Headache didn't want to stand around admiring like everyone else; he wanted to stand beside Tafari and share in the admiration. He seemed to borrow Tafari's borrowed eyes and used them to bear down on Shorty. He stepped to Shorty and asked, "Yo, where you live at, son?!"

"Wha-what?" Shorty stuttered.

"You live on the southside, don't you?!" Shorty nodded, reluctantly.

"We don't like dudes that live on the southside!" Lil' Headache said, his face inches from Shorty's. "Yo, gimme a dollar!" Lil' Headache's hands patted Shorty's pant pockets before stuffing themselves inside. His hands came out of each pocket just as they went in. Empty.

Lil' Headache grabbed two fists full of Shorty's sweatshirt and growled, "I'm takin' this iPod!" Shorty gave it up without putting up a fight. Lil' Headache was staring through Shorty, but said loud enough for everyone to hear, "From now on, anybody that lives on the southside gotta pay rent every Friday! If you ain't got money, we takin' ya jewels, iPods"—he held Shorty's iPod in the air—"and if ya ain't got nothin', ya just gonna take a beat down!"

The southside was where Dready and Donovan lived. Since they robbed Tafari on the train that night, all the guys from the southside had to pay. Tafari and his crew spent the rest of the school day terrorizing boys from the southside by slamming them into the walls and digging out the little bit of change they had in their pockets.

In between one of the classes, Tafari, Los, and Stretch gathered in the boys' restroom to count up the goods.

"I got ten dollars and a watch," Los bragged. "What did y'all get?"

"I got a brand new pair of headphones and eight dollars," Stretch showed off.

"I got five dollars and that gold chain from Donovan's girl," Tafari added.

"I ain't never seen Donovan so scared before," Los admitted. "He's usually the one doin' the robbin'. I'm so glad you down wit' us now, Tafari." Lil' Headache burst through the restroom door, dragging a kicking and screaming Vaughn across the slippery tiles. Stretch helped Lil' Headache scoop him up and pinned him against the wall. Their hands were all over Vaughn's pockets. He must have felt like he was being attacked by an octopus.

Tafari rushed over and intervened. "Chill! Chill! I know him!"

"You know him?" Lil' Headache asked, staring at Tafari strangely.

"Yeah. He's cool," Tafari assured. Lil' Headache and Stretch backed off. Vaughn staggered to his feet and quickly tucked his wrinkled buttoned up shirt back into his pants and dried his eyes with the back of his hands.

"You be hangin' out wit' this cornball?" Lil' Headache said, mean mugging Vaughn.

"Nah, I don't be hangin' out wit' cornballs. You crazy or something?!" Tafari answered quickly. "It's just that his mom and my mom are cool. And if something happens to him, his mom is going tell my mom and then my mom is gonna be beefin' wit' me and I ain't tryna hear that right now." Vaughn had that look in his eyes. A look very familiar to Tafari. Vaughn's eyes narrowed, and Tafari knew it was just a matter of seconds before his mouth erupted like the backed-up toilet bowl behind the stall he was standing in front of and crap all over Tafari's rep.

"I'll be right back," Tafari said, grabbing Vaughn by the arm. "I'ma take him to class so nobody don't mess wit' him."

Walking trough the school's second floor corridor, Vaughn gave Tafari a light shove. "Why you called me a cornball?"

"Nah, I ain't call you a cornball; *they* called you a cornball," Tafari said with a chuckle.

"Yes, you did! You said you don't be hanging out with cornballs!"

"I *had* to say that, man. I got a reputation to protect."

"What reputation?"

"I'm the *man* 'round here," Tafari said, thumping his chest. "People are scared of me."

"Scared of you for what?"

"Some street stuff that went down. You wouldn't understand."

"You mean to tell me, them thugs that was about to rob me in the restroom are afraid of you?"

"Yup."

"They're scared of you, fareal?"

"Yes!"

"They're scared of you, and they called me a cornball, but I beat you up every time we wrestle."

"No, you don't. Get out of here!" Vaughn dropped his backpack to the floor and grabbed Tafari in a headlock. His pipe-cleaner arms were ringing Tafari's neck. It was a bit of a struggle, but Tafari finally managed to wiggle his head free. "Yo, get off me, man! What's wrong witchu?!" Tafari complained, pushing Vaughn away. Tafari straightened out his clothes and quickly scanned the halls hoping nobody was around to see that.

"See, I told you I could beat you," Vaughn bragged, picking up his backpack. "They should be scared of me and calling *you* a cornball."

"Man, you snuck me. I wasn't even ready." Vaughn dropped his backpack again, wanting to show Tafari he was tougher.

"Man, pick up your backpack. I ain't got time for that." Vaughn slipped the straps of his backpack over his shoulders. "What street stuff did you do that got everyone so scared?" Vaughn asked.

"I shot somebody," Tafari stated, proudly.

"You what?!" Vaughn gasped.

"I shot somebody. Well, not just anybody. I shot this thug named Dready who everyone was afraid of. Then I took his chain."

"I don't believe you," Vaughn said, looking at Tafari sideways.

"You ain't gotta believe me," Tafari shrugged. "But why do you think everyone respects me? Why do you think them thugs that were about to rob you, listened to me? Why did they leave you alone when I told 'em to?"

"You fareal? You shot someone?"

"Yup. Right in his leg."

"Why did you shoot him?"

"He was about to shoot me so it was either me or him." Vaughn froze mid-stride and stared at Tafari, strangely. Everyone that Tafari encountered since that infamous night when the gun went off and hit Dready in the leg, looked at him the same way. Except for Vaughn. The look in his eyes were different. "Don't tell anybody about this," Tafari warned, wagging a finger in his face. "Especially not your mother. You know how your mom and my mom like to talk."

"Don't worry," Vaughn assured, waving him off. "I ain't gonna tell nobody." They were interrupted by an explosion of static from the walkie-talkie of a security guard in the nearby staircase. Before one of them overzealous resource officers spotted them, Tafari and Vaughn figured it would be safer to get to their classes immediately.

Chapter 10

Three days later, Tafari and Malikah met up after school and walked hand in hand to the pizza shop.

"Lemme get a slice of pizza with extra cheese, pepperoni, and sausage," Malikah ordered. "And lemme get an extra large Sprite." As Malikah was placing her order, Tafari's brain was calculating the order just as fast as the pudgy man with the red cheeks was punching the keys on the cash register. *Extra cheese, pepperoni, sausage, and a large Sprite?* Tafari thought, his hand in his pocket blindly counting the few singles and loose change.

"And you, sir?" Red Cheeks asked.

"Excuse me?"

"What will you be having?"

"Oh . . . um . . . I'll just have a um . . ." Tafari paused, dipped his hand back into his pocket and fumbled with his change one more time. "I'll just get a small Sprite."

"Small Sprite? That's it?" Malikah asked. "I thought you said you were hungry?" *I am!* Tafari screamed in his head. *Maybe if you didn't order the extra everything and the biggest drink on the menu, I could eat too!* "I just remembered, my mom is cooking my favorite dinner, barbecue chicken, and I don't wanna ruin my appetite," Tafari lied.

Tafari and Malikah took a seat at the booth closest to the door. "I love the way you chew," Tafari said, gazing lovingly into Malikah's warm brown eyes.

"Thank you," Malikah said, a single string of cheese forming a bridge from the pizza in her hand and her small mouth.

"I got something for you," Tafari announced, reaching into his pocket. "Close your eyes." As Malikah squeezed her eyelids together her lips fell apart. Her straight whites were gleaming at Tafari. "Okay, you can open them," Tafari said, his arm outstretched across the table with an open palm.

"Oh my goodness," Malikah gasped, reaching into Tafari's open palm.

"Do you like it?"

"It's beautiful," Malikah chirped, removing the ring from Tafari's hand.

"Is it better than *that* one?" Tafari asked, pointing at the ring that was occupying her ring finger.

"Yes, it's much better. And bigger."

"So, are you gonna take *that* ring off?"

"You take it off for me," Malikah requested, extending her hand to Tafari. Tafari ripped off the ring, nearly taking her finger with it. He slid the new ring onto Malikah's ring finger.

"This ring looks expensive," Malikah said, steadying her left hand in front of her eyes. "How could you afford this?"

"I traded in a gold chain that I . . . found for the ring."

"Thank you so much," Malikah cheered. "I love it." Malikah stood up, reached across the table and threw her arms around Tafari's neck. "So whatchu gon' do with the old ring?" Tafari inquired.

"Keep it," Malikah answered, sitting back down.

"Are you still gonna wear it?"

"No, I don't think so. Maybe I'll take it to the jewelry store and have them melt it down into a pair of earrings or something." Tafari took a satisfying sip of his Sprite, knowing that Malikah's connection with Dready was completely severed.

The door to the pizza shop flew open. Tafari gagged on his Sprite and his heart skipped a beat as the two new customers entered. Tafari knew instantly, the new patrons weren't there for the pizza. They were there for *beef.* With him.

"I told you he was gonna be here with another girl," Vaughn said, turning to Mahogany, who stood beside him. "I told you he was cheatin' on you." Mahogany's mouth and eyes were wide. She studied Tafari's face as if she didn't recognize it. As if she was trying to find the real Tafari somewhere behind the scowl that masked his face.

"Tafari, what's going on here?" Mahogany asked, her voice a mix of surprise and hurt.

"Who are *you*?" Malikah asked, jumping up in Mahogany's face.

"I'm Tafari's girlfriend."

"No you ain't. *I'm* his girl."

"Tafari, is this true?" Mahogany asked, her eyes pleading with Tafari to make sense of the crazy situation. Tafari hesitated; Malikah didn't. "Are you that blind that you can't tell what's goin' on here? Obviously he dumped ya butt and chose me."

"First of all," Mahogany snapped, storms clouds forming in her eyes. "Ain't nobody talking to you."

"Well, I'm talkin' to *you*," Malikah said, finger wagging in Mahogany's face.

"You better get outta my face!"

"Or else?"

"Or else you gonna melt my eyebrows off. Ya breath is hot!"

"Ohhhhhhhh!" sang the boys sitting in the booth behind Tafari.

"Ya *man* didn't have a problem with my breath when we was kissin'!" Malikah snapped off.

"Tafari, you kissed her?" Mahogany gasped.

"Yup," Malikah cut back in. "And it was good." The dark light that illuminated Mahogany's face on the train when she first encountered Dready was back. "Is that what you do?" Mahogany snarled. "Go around kissin' on random boys?"

"If that's what I choose. I can get any *man* that I want."

"That's 'cause you're a dirty little h—"

"Mahogany!" Vaughn interrupted, drowning out the curse Mahogany uttered.

"What did you call me?!" Malikah barked.

"You heard what I said."

"Ya just jealous 'cause you can never in ya wildest dreams be as fly as me," Malikah bragged. "That's right; I'm young, fly, and flashy. My Prada shades cost more than your entire outfit, including those run-over Payless shoes you're wearing." The boys behind Tafari were falling over each other with laughter. Other high schoolers who were sprinkled throughout the pizza shop were twisting in their seats and straining their necks to watch. Malikah wasn't done. "I'm flyer than you, dress better than you, and I got way more guys wanting to get wit' me than you. So don't you ever in ya little ugly life fix ya mouth to say something slick about me wit' ya black self. You so black if you wrapped yourself in plastic you would look like soy sauce." The entire pizza shop erupted with wild laughter, resembling a scene straight from the set of Nick Cannon's *Wild N' Out* after one of the comedians just spit a brilliant one-liner.

Slowly, rage was building throughout Mahogany's body. Tafari noticed her shoulders and chest heaving up and down, building momentum. Without warning, Mahogany lunged at Malikah like a sprinter out of the speed blocks. She struck Malikah in the chest with two open palms, shoving her back into the rickety table, sending her, the pizza, and two cups of soda spilling to the floor. By this time, the man behind the counter had rushed in between Malikah and Mahogany.

"Not in my shop!" he shouted, hands spread like wings to keep the combatants apart. "Take that ghetto nonsense outside where it belongs!"

Tafari grabbed Malikah by her arm, keeping her from charging at Mahogany. "Get off me!" Malikah yelled at Tafari before turning her attention to Mahogany. "You better watch ya back! You better watch ya back!"

"I'm right here!" Mahogany yelled back. "You all talk! You ain't gonna do nothin'."

"I'ma see you again. Watch!" Malikah shouted at Mahogany. "You a bum! You dirty! You dirty!" Vaughn pushed Mahogany through the doors and they disappeared in the crowd. A sense of guilt clouded Tafari's chest when he replayed the scene in his mind's eye. He felt like he was responsible for Mahogany acting so out of character. The weight of shame was heavy on his shoulders as he slumped down into a seat, figuring that Mahogany probably would never want to speak to him again.

Chapter 11

Several weeks came and went, and Tafari was still doing the same things. Still skipping Bible study to hang on the corner with his crew. Still robbing southside boys in the school restrooms and corridors, and pawning their goods to buy Malikah more jewelry. And still avoiding Mahogany since encountering her at the pizza shop.

It was a little after 9:00 p.m., which was the time Mom usually expected him home from Bible study. Tafari rolled his bike off the elevator and leaned it against the wall on the sixth floor. Tafari was pulling his sweater over his head as he walked up the steps and pushed through the door onto the roof top. He blindly reached down for his backpack and grabbed a fist full of air. Tafari looked down to confirm what his fist already knew. There was nothing but air there. But how could that be?

Three hours earlier, his backpack was there. A little before 6:00 p.m., Tafari stripped off his Bible study clothes as the sun watched and stuffed them into his backpack. He left the bag on the side of the door while he hung out with his boys on the corner. But three hours later, his backpack was missing.

Tafari searched every corner of the roof top and still didn't see anything but air. He knew that addicts would sometimes go to the roofs to use drugs. And he also knew that they would steal anything that wasn't nailed down to sell it for money to buy drugs. But what could a drug addict get for a worn white dress shirt, some slacks and some old Church shoes? Tafari headed down stairs, trying to figure out how he could sneak into his room without Mom seeing him in his street clothes. He opened the staircase door and shock froze him in the doorway. The black backpack was dangling from Mom's hand as she stood in the doorway of his apartment with the door resting on her back.

Her face winced at the sight of Tafari, as if she were in pain. When Mom stepped toward Tafari, Vaughn poked his head out of the door. Tafari knew immediately how his backpack ended up in Mom's hands.

"Why are you wearing those hoodlum clothes?!" Mom asked, looking at her son as if she didn't recognize him. While Tafari was thinking of a lie, Mom's hand was in and out of his backpack, pulling out his white shirt and pants. "And why are your good clothes balled up in this backpack?!" She snapped, waving the clothes at him. Tafari's mouth opened but nothing came out. "Huh?! I'm talking to you Tafari. Answer me!" Mom insisted. Vaughn was standing behind Mom with that stupid grin on is face. The same grin Vaughn wore when he stood by while Tafari was being reprimanded by Ms. Morehead.

"Because those clothes are for cornballs!" Tafari snapped, his eyes rolling up and down Vaughn's attire which was similar to the clothes Mom had balled up in her hands.

"What?" Mom said, confusion wrinkling her brow.

"Cornballs! Those clothes are for punks!" Vaughn wasn't laughing anymore.

"Punks?!" Mom scoffed. "These are God's clothes! Ain't no reason to be ashamed wearing these clothes."

"Well, I almost got killed wearing God's clothes!"

"What are you talking about?"

"Not too long ago a Jamaican dude pulled out a gun on me while I was on the train wearing *those* clothes."

"Oh my God! Why didn't you tell me?"

"Tell you for what? What were you gon' do?"

"Tafari!"

"It's true. Whenever you think there's a problem with me, all you do is pray."

"Well, I sure can't call your father because God knows where he is. It's not easy being a single mom trying to raise a son. So you tell me since you have all the answers, what am I supposed to do? Huh?"

"You ain't gotta do nothing. I can take care of myself now."

"Oh, so you a *man* now? You got your little street-hood-lum clothes and you think that makes you a man now?"

"Ain't nobody pulled a gun on me since I put on these clothes."

"Yeah, but *you* pulled out a gun on somebody and shot them," Vaughn called out. Mom's face nearly fell apart. She put her hand to her mouth as if that would hold it together.

"You a liar!" Tafari yelled. "Ma, he's lyin'!"

"So why did you tell me you shot somebody?"

"I was just messin' witchu."

"I don't believe you."

"Shut up and mind ya business!"

"Alright, stop all that yellin'!" Mom yelled, before turning back to Tafari. "And by the way, Vaughn tells me that you haven't gone to Bible study in over a month. Where have you been?"

"I . . . um . . . just been around."

"Around, like on the streets?! The same streets I told you to stay away from?!" Tafari didn't answer. Mom turned to Vaughn. "I think it's time for you to go home, because me and Tafari got bigger issues to talk about right now." Vaughn hugged Mom and headed for the elevator.

"Snitches get stitches," Tafari grumbled as Vaughn circled around him toward the elevator.

"You threatening me, Tafari?!" Vaughn said, loud enough for Mom to hear.

"Did you threaten him?" Mom asked, fury in her eyes. "Huh? What did you say to him, Tafari?"

"He said snitches get stitches," Vaughn answered for him.

"Did you say that, Tafari?"

"No."

"Yes, you did!" Vaughn refuted.

"You know what, Tafari, you are out of control! Get your butt in this apartment, now!" Tafari glared at Vaughn as he entered the elevator. Mom stepped aside as Tafari squeezed into the obscure apartment. The way the iron door slammed and locked behind him, Tafari felt as if he had just entered a prison cell. His gut was twisting into knots. It was as if his gut was warning him that the night was only going to get worse.

Tafari walked slowly as if an executioner was waiting on him at the end of the hall. He froze at the kitchen entrance where an opening of light cut through the darkened hall. Tafari realized instantly that there wasn't just one executioner waiting on him; there were five. Ms. Green and her twin sons, Noel and Leon, Josiah, and a lady that he recognized from church, probably Josiah's mom, sat around the kitchen table. They all even wore dark colors. Noel and Leon played the role of sympathetic executioners. Tafari saw pain in their broken faces and sorrow in their eyes. Their eyes seemed to be apologizing to Tafari for what was about to go down. Those same eyes also seemed to tell Tafari there wasn't anything they could do to save him. Or themselves.

There was no hint of sorrow in Ms. Green's stone face. She was glaring at Tafari as if she couldn't wait to prop his neck on a guillotine and slice his head smooth off. Josiah and his mom also glared at Tafari. Josiah's eyes were a lot different than they were the last time Tafari saw him when he was pleading for his life on the side of the church. Tafari figured the momma's boy all of a sudden felt tough because he was sitting next to his mommy.

Tafari's mother circled around him, unfolded a folding chair, took a seat, and joined the parents in a glaring contest.

The kitchen was quiet. So quiet that Tafari could hear the light hum of the refrigerator. He could even hear his nose dragging in air and pushing it back out. But the hard glares from the parents' eyes were the loudest in the silence.

"Do you know why we're all here?" Mom broke the silence.

"No," Tafari said, playing dumb.

"We're here because my boys got expelled from school because they were trying to be like you," Ms. Green said, her words stinging Tafari like a slap to the face.

"Whatchu talkin' about?"

"They been sneaking a change of clothes with them to school and changing in the restrooms into clothes that look like what you're wearing now. They been skipping classes. And the final straw was when they got caught by a teacher with a toy gun that looked like the real thing. They were using it to rob students of their lunch money in the school staircases. That's when they got expelled. Now, I have to find another junior high school for them to go to in order to finish up eighth grade," Ms. Green paused to dry her eyes. "And it's all your fault."

"How is it my fault? I ain't tell 'em to dress like me or bring a toy gun to school to rob nobody."

"You might as well have," Ms. Green growled, eyes shooting daggers at Tafari. "They look up to you. They been watching you and copying you. Everything that they done in school is what they seen you do. Or what you told them *you* did. If you would have told them that your goal was to be valedictorian of your school, my boys would have locked themselves in their bedrooms, studying up a storm. But you chose to be a . . . a . . . street hoodlum."

"I'm only sixteen," Tafari stated. "If your sons are looking up to me and not you, then it sounds like you need to do a better job at being a mother." Everyone in the kitchen gasped. They couldn't believe what Tafari said. Tafari couldn't believe what he said either. But it was too late. The refrigerator seemed to hum a little louder. Air was thicker in his nostrils.

"Tafari, you apologize to Ms. Green, right now!" Mom demanded. Tafari wanted to, but his tongue wouldn't move. The words wouldn't form and nothing came out of his mouth.

"That's alright, Ms. King," Ms. Green said, waving Mom off. "The streets got a serious hold on that boy. That boy needs some serious prayer."

"Forget prayer," Josiah's mom said, popping out of her seat. "If somebody doesn't put a strap to the back of that boy's legs, I will." She pulled an old tattered belt from her worn pocketbook and approached Tafari.

Mom jumped up and impeded her progress. "If anybody is gonna put hands on my boy, it's gonna be me." Tafari took a step back, stunned at the lady's courage.

"Are we gonna talk about how that hoodlum over there stole my son's bike?" Josiah's mom asked, shaking the belt at Tafari.

"Tafari, did you take Josiah's bike?" Mom asked.

"N-no," Tafari stammered. "He said I could get a ride."

"He's lying!" Josiah yelled out, half of his face hidden behind his mom's shoulder.

"You've had his bike for three weeks," Josiah's mom yelled at Tafari. "That's the longest ride I ever heard of!"

"And he pulled a gun out on me too," Josiah added, only his left eye was visible just over his mom's shoulder.

"Tafari! You have a gun?!" Mom gasped, again.

"No!"

"Yes, he does," a voice behind Josiah's mom called out. "He was going to shoot me beside the church."

"That's not true," Tafari lied.

"Where's the gun, Tafari?"

"I don't have a gun." Mom plunged her hand in Tafari's backpack and her hand swam around in the bottom of the bag. Tafari's heart skipped a beat. Tafari studied the outline of his backpack for any type of lump shaped like a gun. Then he tested his memory, trying to remember if he put the gun in the bag earlier that evening. Mom's hand came out as it went in. Empty. That's when Tafari realized he left the gun in his boot box under his bed.

"My son ain't a liar!" Josiah's mom contested. "If my son says you pulled out a gun on him, I believe him! Ms. King, I'm sorry; if you're not going to do anything about this, I'm calling the cops myelf."

"Cops?! Why are we getting the cops involved?" Mom asked, confusion and pain in her voice.

"Did you not hear what my son said? He said *your son* pulled out a gun on him. A gun! God forbid the gun went off. Then what?" Josiah's mom dried her eyes with her finger tips.

"Tafari, what in the world has gotten into you?! I didn't raise you like this at all! You better tell me who gave you the gun and where the gun is now, or I will do the unthinkable and call the cops on my only son!"

"Why you yellin' at me?!" Tafari yelled back at Mom. "I said I don't have a gun! Why don't you believe your own son?!"

"Because my own son has been lying to me!" Mom responded. "Had me thinking you were going to Bible study when instead you've been hanging in the streets! Walking out of here in one set of clothes, only to change into them hoodlum clothes! How can I believe you when you've been living a lie?"

"You don't get it!" Tafari said, waving her off. "You just don't understand!"

"Don't be talking to your mother like that, boy!" Josiah's mom cut in.

"Wasn't anybody talking to you," Tafari lashed out.

"Tafari, you apologize, now!" Mom shouted. All of a sudden, Ms. Green and Josiah's mom started yelling at Tafari at the same time. Mom joined the incoherent yelling match. They were yelling so loud, it was hard for him to make out what they were saying. Three parents, shoulder to shoulder to shoulder, their faces twisted in anger, fingers wagging, yelling, growling, and cursing as they crept toward Tafari, closing in on his face. Tafari had had enough. Felt like a trapped rat and needed to escape the heat of the kitchen.

"I'm outta here!" Tafari announced, throwing his hands up in the air before rushing toward the door.

"Tafari, don't you dare walk out of this house!" Mom called out. Too late. Those were the last words Tafari heard before the door slammed shut. He grabbed his bike from the staircase, carried it down the six flights of stairs, and rolled out of the building.

Tafari cocked his head back, peered deep into the dark heavens and let out a primitive yell deep from his core to empty out the anger that filled in his gut. He rode his bike deep into the heart of the projects, pedaling hard, back teeth grinding into each other even harder, tears leaping off of his face and into the driving wind. Tafari's brain raced as fast as the spinning spokes in his wheels while trying to figure out whose pillow he was going to rest his head on that night. He certainly wasn't going to lay his head on the old Power Ranger pillow case on his single bed. After the way he stormed out of his apartment, there was no way he was going back that night.

Just up ahead, Tafari spotted Lil' Headache's building. He figured he could sleep over at Lil' Headache's apartment at least for one night until things cooled down at his place.

Chapter 12

Tafari squeezed on the hand brakes and his bike screeched to a halt just outside of his building. He hadn't stepped a Timberland foot in that building since he stormed out of his apartment three nights earlier with Mom, Ms. Green, and Josiah's mom all yelling at him. Tafari looked up and eyed the Power Ranger bed sheets that covered his bedroom window, remembering a time when those sheets would cover him while he lay on his back on his twin size mattress. He had dreams about that old mattress while he tossed and turned on the cold floor in Lil' Headache's bedroom on the first night, tossed and turned some more on the hard rug in Stretch's bedroom on the second night, and while he slept on the inflatable mattress that wouldn't inflate in Los's bedroom on the third night. Tafari had worn out his welcome at his friends' apartments and was hoping to get a good night's sleep on his own bed.

He rolled his bike into the elevator, kicked the kickstand down, and pressed the button for six. When the elevator door dragged open, he rolled his bike towards apartment 6C and stopped in front of his door, inhaling the stale hallway air. Tafari searched his pockets for his keys but couldn't find them. He raised his hand and was about to knock on the door but his fingers fell apart just as soon as they balled up. He couldn't do it. He wasn't so sure he wanted to face his mother yet. What would he say to her? What would she say to him?

Tafari turned around and walked his bike down the dimly lit hallway and pushed in the door to the stairwell. His face cringed as a breeze of stale urine rushed into his face while carrying the bike to the top step. He leaned the bike against the dingy white concrete wall and took a seat on the top step. Teams of lies and excuses gathered on the center stage of his brain and engaged in an ultimate debate to see which one could make the most sense and be singled out and presented to his mom as a ticket in the door. After minutes of going back and forth, none made sense to Tafari. At least not enough to fool his mom into believing he never had a gun and Josiah's mom was just some crazy lady that didn't know what she was talking about.

Tafari's eyelids were heavy and his body was growing weary. He tipped over and made a concrete bed out of the top step platform. Tafari clapped his palms together as if he was praying and then lay on his side with his hands under the side of his face like a pillow. A cold breeze needled up his back from underneath the red door that separated the bed from the roof as he slipped into a light sleep.

The block was unusually quiet. Tafari was chillin' on the corner and felt droplets of water pelting him on top of his hoody. He removed his hoody, looked up, and saw water streaming through cracks of the building he was leaning on. The building snapped and cracked like an old rickety house before it crumbled under the pressure and a waterfall came crashing down on top of him, burying him beneath the deep water. Each time Tafari's gaping mouth emerged from the raging water to suck a mouthful of air, giant waves, shaped like greenish-blue fists were pounding the top his head, shoving him back under the water. Tafari flailed, wildly, and spotted his gun again. He grabbed at it but it dissolved in his hands, unable to save him. Off in the distance was his rhyme book, about as big as a branch, gliding toward him like a canoe. Tafari's head bobbed in and out of the water as he fought off the waves that were grabbing at his legs, trying to yank him beneath the surface. Water plugged up his nose and streamed into his mouth, strangling the scream in his throat. The book moved to within arms reach giving Tafari one last chance to save his self. He reached for it . . .

Tafari snapped out of his sleep, sitting up on the top step, and realized he was dreaming.

Every Saturday morning, as far as he could remember, the aroma of turkey sausages would soak through the door of 6A and bathe the stale air in the hall. It would even leak under the door of 6C while he was a few feet away in the kitchen, eating a big bowl of Lucky Charms. The scent would tempt him to dump the bowl of magically delicious cereal in the toilet and knock on Ms. Green's door with a plate and fork. Or at least shake his mom awake and beg her to do what seemed to be against her religion: cook on Saturdays. They often ate take-out from Lee's Kitchen.

But on that Saturday morning, it wasn't turkey sausages that filled the halls. It was a different aroma. Smelled like dinner. Like chicken and ziti or something similar. Tafari stood up rubbing boogers out of his eyes with his knuckles and massaging his sore left shoulder.

Tafari's stomach was churning because he wasn't moving toward the source of the sauce fast enough. He entered the hall and his nose knew immediately it wasn't coming from 6A. The aroma was stronger down the hall near the door that faced him straight ahead. That was strange because 6C was never responsible for filling the halls with aromas like that, especially not on no Saturday morning.

Tafari heard the locks pop to his apartment and the door slowly inched open. In his mind, Tafari saw himself spin his bike around and duck into the stairwell. Outside of his mind he was frozen in his stance like Frosty. He couldn't move.

As the door opened, a pool of light flooded into the hall and a small figure appeared in the doorway. With radiant light behind it, it looked as if a small shadow had peeled itself off of a wall somewhere and was walking out of his apartment. The black shadow stepped into the hall, carrying a full black garbage bag. Tafari's eyes were photography lenses trying to adjust to the light. The shadowy figure was starting to look familiar. Her once familiar housecoat and almost matching slippers weren't so familiar anymore. The brightness of the tan had faded to a sickly pale and her once fuzzy slippers resembled the matted-down dingy look of the stray, collarless mutts that hang around the garbage bin behind Lee's kitchen. It had only been four nights since the last time he saw his mom but she looked . . . *different*. Looked smaller to him. Looked like she aged, too. Tafari figured that was the first time he had really *looked* at Mom in a long time.

Mom's eyes widened and her lips quivered as if Tafari's presence startled her. Her eyes remained wide and her lips began to bend into a smile. Before the smile could reach its peak, her wide eyes shrunk into slits, and her smile started bending the other way. "What are you doing here?" Mom asked, coldly.

"I . . . um . . . just wanted to see how you were doin'," Tafari stammered.

"I'm fine," Mom said, her voice cracking. "How are you?"

"Okay, I guess."

"Where have you been?" Mom croaked.

"I was staying with some friends." Mom tried to say something but her face cracked. That first expression reappeared. Her lip quivered again, but more intense. More like a shake. Tears burst from her eyes and washed down her face. She covered her mouth with her hands and deep, throaty sobs erupted from behind her fingers. Her little body crumbled and nearly collapsed where she stood. Tafari was quick enough to catch her just before she landed on top of the garbage bag. He walked her into the kitchen and helped her into a seat at the head of the wooden kitchen table. Tafari handed her a plastic cup of faucet water and stood aside as she sipped and sobbed. Sobbed and sipped, until the water and the sobs had all but disappeared.

She stared blankly again, as if something was holding her mind's eye's attention. Tafari hesitated to say anything because he didn't want to see her erupt into a bunch of tears and sobs again. While she stared at the refrigerator, Tafari stared at the chicken that was sizzling under a pool of grease in the frying pan on top of the greasy stove. He glanced at the big pots on the back of the stove with steam spraying out from under the pot covers. Tafari noticed the other pots lined up on the cabinet with dried gravy and grease stains tearing down the sides. He removed the top off of one of the pots and stuck his nose over it.

"Get your filthy hands out of my pots!" Mom spat, still staring at the fridge.

Tafari slammed the lid back onto the pot and stuck his hands under the kitchen faucet. "And don't wash your ole' nasty hands in the kitchen sink, either," Mom spat again. Tafari glared at Mom before he started toward the bathroom which was right next door to his old bedroom.

"What happened to my son?" Mom asked, just before Tafari exited the kitchen. Their eyes connected and danced together for a minute. Hers were filled with water; Tafari's were filled with curiosity. He wondered what was stirring up under that water, behind those eyes.

"Whatchu mean?" Tafari asked.

"This ain't my son," Mom said, her eyes and hand waving up and down Tafari's body. "My son doesn't dress like a street hoodlum. My son doesn't get into any trouble. My son never lied to me. I used to be so proud of my son. My son used to dress so nice, go to church and Bible study. My son was sweet and innocent. Other parents would compliment me on how well I was raising my son. They would even ask me for parenting tips to help their out-of-control sons. But when Ms. Jones showed up at my door with her son, Josiah, and told me you stole his bike and pointed a gun at him, I was shocked and couldn't believe they were talking about my son. I never, ever saw this coming. You have become the talk of the church and not in a good way. I was so embarrassed that I didn't go to church this past Sunday. So please, Tafari, help me understand. What happened to my son?"

"You don't know what ya son been through," Tafari answered.

"What could you have possibly gone through?" Mom asked. "I thought I was keeping you safe by keeping you away from the streets and not letting you go outside late at night. The only time I let you go out was to go to Bible study."

"Well, one night after Bible study, I walked Mahogany home and got jumped because I don't live on that side of the projects. Then another night, on my way home from Bible study, I got a gun put in my face and was stripped of all of my clothes. And then another night, on my way to Bible study I was about to get thrown off the roof until I spit some hot rhymes that saved my life." Mom sat in stunned silence.

"If you really wanted to save me from the streets," Tafari snickered, "maybe you should have handcuffed me to the radiator like those psycho parents do to their children."

"This isn't a joking matter, Tafari," Mom snapped. "I had no idea these things were happening to you. Why didn't you tell me?"

"If I told you, what were you gonna do besides pray for me?" Tafari asked, rhetorically. "What I'm goin' through right now is way different than the problems I had when I was little. Remember when I was seven years old and we were at the playground and I was wrestling in the grass. Then all of a sudden it got serious and that bully had my face in the grass and you ran over and snatched the bully off of me."

"Yeah, I remember," Mom said. "That girl could fight." Mom and Tafari laughed together, cutting through the tension.

"Well, I'm sixteen now and my problems are way bigger than me getting beat up by some fat girl," Tafari explained. "You can't rescue me from these thugs I'm dealing with now. If you tried, they ain't gonna run off crying like that girl did. They will put a gun in ya face if you put your hands on them."

"So, what am I supposed to do?"

"I can take care of myself. You don't have to do anything."

"I cannot just sit back and allow you to continue to lie to me. I cannot just sit back and allow you to play with guns. And I cannot allow you to run around on them streets while I sit back and pray that you don't get killed."

"I'm not gonna get killed, Mom."

"Running around on these streets is like playing Russian roulette. It's just a matter of time. The only way off the streets is either in handcuffs or a casket."

"That's not true. I could stop hanging out with my friends whenever I want with no problems," Tafari said, not sure if he believed his own words.

"I'm sure Timothy Morgan thought just like you do."

"Timothy Morgan? What does he have to do with anything?"

"You didn't hear?"

"Hear what?"

"Timothy was killed a couple of nights ago on the streets."

"Little Timothy?"

"Yes."

"Timothy that used to sit behind me in church and next to me in English class? What happened?"

"Same thing that happened with you. He started skipping church and playing hooky from school to hang out on the streets with his new friends. From what I was told, there was a shootout the other night and he was shot and killed in the crossfire. He was an innocent bystander. He was hanging out on the corner when he should have been at choir practice." Mom paused to clear her throat and wipe her eyes with her finger tips. "I'm going over to his apartment a little bit later to pay my respects."

"Is that what the food is for?" Tafari asked.

"Yes."

"Aren't you supposed to bring flowers or something?"

"No, food is usually what people bring to those who are grieving. It's a way to provide comfort and show that we care. Plus, the last thing Mrs. Morgan wants to do is cook."

Mom rose out of her seat and moved to the stove. The stove was tucked between the sink and the L-shaped cabinets about three feet from the square wooden table that sat in the middle of the kitchen floor. She grabbed a fork from the dish rack and began turning the chicken. Grease popped out of the frying pan and onto the sleeves of her robe. After turning the chicken, Mom reached for a torn envelop from the cabinet, removed the folded letter, and returned back to her seat. "I received this letter from your school the other day."

"What does it say?"

"It says that you have had an excessive amount of tardies and that you have been cutting classes. It says that you have been selected to attend the S.I.C.K. mentoring program at Bronx High. You are required to attend the classes every day after school for two weeks. If you do not attend the mentoring classes, then you will be suspended from school for three days because of the tardies and cutting classes."

"I rather be suspended than attend some lame mentoring classes."

"You don't have a choice," Mom said. "You are attending the mentoring program because I do not want you to have the suspension on your permanent record."

"I wonder what I'm gonna have to do there?"

"They are going to be mentoring you and hopefully teaching you how to make good decisions. I always knew the day would come when you would need a male in your life to teach you how to be a man since God knows where your father is. Hopefully, this program can fill the void left by your father being absent."

"How do you know the mentor is gonna be a man?"

"It says here that a Mr. Sekou will be the mentor in charge. Do you know him?"

"Yeah, he's my English teacher."

"Well, it seems like you have a positive, African American male teacher at your school that wants to mentor you," Mom said, standing up and walking back over to the stove. "All these young boys are dying on the streets because they don't have fathers at home to guide them. I don't know what's going on in this neighborhood anymore, but I do know you have a great opportunity to get some guidance from a man and I really want you to go."

Tafari stared absently at Mom as she stabbed the chicken legs with a fork and placed them onto sheets of napkins that lined the glass plate. Visions of the last time he saw Timothy chilled the back of his neck and arms. *I just saw him the other day*, Tafari thought. *And just like that, he's gone.* Tafari really didn't want to go but he figured with all the heartache he had caused Mom over the last week it was the least he could do for her.

Chapter 13

The bell blared through the halls and classrooms of Bronx High, indicating the end of the school day. As students hurried through the exits, Tafari descended to the first floor, following the signs for the S.I.C.K. meeting. The signs led him to the band room just around the corner from the gym. Carefully and suspiciously, Tafari crept into the room. He froze at the entrance when he saw three students sitting at the tablet arm desks. They were spread out in the spacious room, one boy sitting in the very back by the piano, another sitting by the window on the far right, and the other sitting in the middle. Tafari slumped into the seat closest to the door just as Mr. Sekou entered.

"Good afternoon, gentlemen!" Mr. Sekou cheered. Nobody responded. "Well," Mr. Sekou continued. "I am

Mr. Sharif Sekou, tenth grade English teacher, and I want to formally welcome you guys to the inauguration of the S.I.C.K. mentoring program. S.I.C.K. stands for Saving Inner City Kids. This is my program; it's a vision I've had for over a decade, and I'm happy to finally get it off the ground. Ever since I graduated college, it's always been my dream to mentor kids who come from the projects. This is just the beginning; my vision is for this program to grow into the communities and beyond." Mr. Sekou's excitement was met with scowls and yawns. "Okay, now that you guys know me, it's time for me to get to know you," Mr. Sekou said, before connecting eyes with Tafari. "So, Tafari King, tell everyone why you are here."

"I'm here because I cut some classes and I have some tardies."

"So what were you doing while you were cutting these classes?"

"Hangin' out in the halls with my peoples. Or we would leave school and hang out on the corner and just chill."

"That's what I'm talkin' about," the boy by the window called out. "Anything is better than sittin' in these borin' classes wit' these borin' teachers."

"Are you Myles Miller?" Mr. Sekou asked, looking down at the clipboard.

"Yup."

"Myles, I'm going to ask you to remove your hood." Myles reluctantly removed the oversized hoody from his head, revealing his wild afro. "So, Myles, why are *you* here?"

"I got a letter in the mail."

"I know that, Myles. *I* sent the letter. But why did you get into trouble?"

"Because I cursed out Mrs. Yeager."

"You cursed her out?"

"Yeah."

"Why did you curse her out?"

"Because she can't teach and she can't control her class."

"What do you mean?"

"Everyone in the class was talkin' and some were throwin' paper balls at each other and she turned around and yelled, 'Myles, be quiet!' So, I yelled back, 'Why you tellin' me to be quiet? What about everybody else?' Then she tries to get crunk and says, 'I'm not talkin' to everybody else. I'm talkin' to you!' Now my boys who were sittin' next to me are laughin' and clownin' me and I ain't havin' that so I said, 'And I'm talkin' to you!' Then she shook her head and said, 'Clearly, ya mother didn't teach you any manners.' Now the whole class is *ohhhin'* and *ahhhin'* and I'm steaming. She had no business talkin' 'bout my mother. So I said, 'That's why you can't teach and nobody likes you, you old bat!'"

"No, you didn't," Mr. Sekou interrupted.

"Yup, I sure did. Then she said, 'I'm gonna write a re-ferral,' and I said, 'I don't give a . . . *freak*,' but I didn't say *freak*. I actually said the other word but I don't wanna disrespect you, Mr. Sekou. So, after that, she wrote me up and now I'm here."

"Now, Myles, was all of that necessary?"

"No, but she brought it on herself. I mean, yeah, I was talkin', but why did she have to single me out when everybody else was talkin too? Then, to make matters worse, she disrespected my mother."

"Teachers aren't perfect," Mr. Sekou reasoned. "She had a class of thirty rowdy students. She was probably frustrated with all the noise and craziness and when she turned around, you were the first person she saw talking and she called you out."

"But that's not fair."

"You're right, it's not fair. But teachers are human, too. We make mistakes. She shouldn't have said anything about your mother; that was wrong. But that doesn't give you the right to curse at her. I mean, you didn't say that curse word to me."

"Because I respect you, Mr. Sekou. I don't respect her. She can't control her class and it's impossible to learn anything in there. That's why I'm failin'. That's why half of the class is failin'. All she does is yell at the students or just ignore us. She's always sayin', 'I can't wait 'til 3:00 so I can go home.' If she hates kids so much, why does she bother to teach?"

"Well, I can't speak for Mrs. Yeager, and to be honest I really don't want to get into it right now because it's taking us off track. My only suggestion to you would be to speak to her one on one after class, and let her know how you feel."

"She never listens to us. Every time one of us tries to talk to her, she brushes us off or just straight ignores us."

"Well, like I said, Myles, this program is to help you guys, not to talk about Mrs. Yeager." Mr. Sekou looked down at his clipboard. "Trevor Burkes." The boy in the middle threw his hand in the air. "Why are you here, Trevor?" Mr. Sekou asked.

"Call me Big Snacks," he insisted.

"Big Snacks?"

"Yeah, my friends call me Big Snacks 'cause, as you can see, I'm big and I always got a snack on me." At that point, Big Snacks removed a Hershey bar from his pocket, ripped off the wrapper, and took a huge bite.

"You ain't big; you fat. They should call you Fat Snacks!" the boy in the very back of the room called out. Everyone laughed. Big Snacks bit his lip in anger, slammed his open palms against the desk, pushed up, and snapped, "You tryna roast?"

"Yeah, that's right! Whatcha gon' do about it, fat boy?"

"Fat boy?!"

"Yeah, you heard me!"

"Yo, I'll come back there and—"

"Hey! Hey! Hey!" Mr. Sekou barked. "Calm down and have a seat! I'm not havin' that type of behavior in here! This is your second chance. Y'all wanna blow it already?"

Both boys sat back down. "Now," Mr. Sekou began, calming his tone. "Big Snacks, why are you here?"

"I don't know. I was hopin' you would tell me," Big Snacks said, mouth full of Hershey.

"Well, it says here that you were a part of a crew that jumped a boy after school on school grounds."

"I ain't touch him," Big Snacks replied.

"So tell me what happened."

"The bell rang and I had just walked out the school doors and I was on my way home when two of my friends came up to me. They said they had beef wit' some dude and asked me to go wit' them to confront the kid. So, we go behind the school and they walked up to this kid that I didn't know. Next thing I know, they started beatin' him up. I kinda felt bad for him but I just stood there. I swear, I ain't touch him."

"If you didn't' touch him, how did you end up getting suspended?"

"Well, the next day, I'm sittin' in History class and Mr. Sullivan, the A.P., comes and gets me. He takes me to the office and when we get there I see two boys already waiting outside the door and the boy who got beat up was sitting on a chair by his desk."

"And then what?"

"So, we walk into the office and Mr. Sullivan makes us stand against the wall, you know, like those police line ups where the suspects have to stand behind the glass except there wasn't no glass in that office. Anyway, Mr.

Sullivan asks the boy to point at the boys who jumped him and he points at me."

"What about the other two boys?"

"Mr. Sullivan lets them go because they had nothing to do wit' it."

"So what happened to your friends? The boy couldn't identify them?"

"Nah, they were wearing hoodies when they beat him up. They didn't get called down to the office."

"So, your friends, the ones who actually beat the kid up, got away with it, but you, who just stood there and didn't touch him, got into trouble?"

"Yup."

"Why didn't you tell Mr. Sullivan you had nothing to do with it?"

"I tried to tell Mr. Sullivan, but he goes into this nonsense about if my friend robbed a bank and I was in the car then I would get arrested too. He said somethin' about me being an accessory."

"It's true."

"But it ain't fair."

"Why didn't you give Mr. Sullivan the names of the boys who actually did it?"

"I ain't a snitch."

"So instead of telling the truth, you'd rather be punished for something you didn't do?"

"I don't really wanna be punished for something I didn't do, but like I said, I ain't a snitch. You ever heard of the statement, 'snitches get stitches'?"

"Yes. I'm very familiar with it."

"Nowadays, its 'snitches get ditches'!" The boy in the back called out. "Snitches get no respect and they always gotta watch their back when they're on the streets. Ain't nobody tryna live like that."

Mr. Sekou looked down at his clipboard. "Angel De La Rosa?"

"That's me, the one and only," Angel stated, proudly.

"And you're here because . . ."

"Y'all teachers are always hatin' on me."

"Why do you think the teachers are always hatin' on you?"

"Because I'ma fly dude."

"I see you think very highly of yourself."

"Somebody has to," Angel bragged. "All I got is me, and if I don't think highly of myself, who else will?"

Mr. Sekou smirked to himself as he glanced at the clipboard again. "It says here that you were caught taggin' the boys' restroom. Do you think that was the right thing to do?"

"Maaaan!" Angel shouted, flaring his hands in the air. "What's the point of this class? This is lame!"

"If it wasn't for this class, you would be home right now on a two-day suspension. Is that what you want?"

"Yeah. At least I'd be home chillin'. Doin' what I wanna do, know what 'm sayin'?"

"Chillin' with a suspension on your school record. Plus, when you were to return from your suspension, you were scheduled to serve three days of in-school suspension."

"I could handle it. It's nothin'."

"You're right about *nothin'*. Because that's exactly what you would learn from all of this. *Nothin'*. In the past, when you guys got in trouble at this school and had to serve in-school suspension, what was that like?"

"It's boring," Myles answered. "We have to stay in the I.S.S. room and sit in this cubicle thing so we can't see or talk to any of the other students. We stay there the whole school day and do our work until the end of the school day and then we leave."

"Exactly. You guys get into trouble and there is no type of remediation going on. The S.I.C.K. program was designed for the at-risk teens in this school that are constantly getting into trouble and are on a *Rule 12* or are about to be on one. This program allows students an opportunity to discuss their problems with someone who can understand them and hopefully come up with solutions to prevent you guys from getting into trouble again."

"What's a Rule 12?" Myles asked.

"A Rule 12 is for students who chronically disrupt or repeatedly violate school rules. A Rule 12 only applies after remediation attempts, including a behavioral correction plan. If you get into trouble while on a Rule 12, then you will be charged and will have to go to a discipline hearing. If you are found guilty, then you get paneled or expelled from the school."

"But I'm not on a Rule 12 or even close to being on one. I've only been in trouble a couple of times," Myles revealed.

"I'm not on a Rule 12, either," Tafari added.

"Not all students who attend my program will be on a Rule 12," Mr. Sekou mentioned. "Sometimes I'll add a student to this class who I feel just stepped on the wrong path and could be headed to a Rule 12 down the road. A student like Tafari. Or I might get a recommendation from a fellow teacher or an A.P. about students who are really good kids but had a really, really bad day. Students like Myles and Big Snacks. Or, I might get a student who—"

"A student who is really on a Rule 12, like me!" Angel called out from the back. At that moment, Ms. Camara, lead guidance counselor, stuck her head in the door.

"Excuse me," Mr. Sekou announced before stepping out of the door.

"This teacher is lame," Angel announced. "He said we can discuss our problems with someone who understands us. Yeah, right. He don't know nothin' about the streets."

"I know right," Myles responded. "I just wanna get this over wit'." Mr. Sekou reentered the room. "Sorry for the interruption," he began, picking up a dry erase marker and walking over to the white board. "So, where do you guys see yourselves in ten years?" Aside from Tafari shifting in his seat, nobody moved. "Don't everyone speak at once," Mr. Sekou joked. "Come on, Angel, in ten years, what will you be doing?"

"Hopefully breathin'," Angel laughed.

"Lets get serious, Angel," Mr. Sekou demanded.

"I am serious. It's real out in them streets. Teens are dyin' every day out there."

"You're right. But if you had a dream, it could—"

"Dreams?" Angel interrupted. "Dreams are for them suckers that get popped in the streets and lose their lives. They're too busy wit' their heads in the clouds dreamin' about tomorrow when they should have been strapped up and payin' attention to today. If they would have been focused on the here and now they might still be alive. All we got is today, that's it. Forget tomorrow."

"Angel, I understand where you comin' from, trust me, I been there" Mr. Sekou said. "Have you ever heard of the saying, 'he who fails to plan is planning to fail'? If you take the time to plan ahead, then you can get out of the projects."

"My brother said there's two ways outta the projects," Angel pointed out. "Either in handcuffs or a casket. And my brother made it out—in a casket, God bless the dead." Angel crossed himself like Catholics do after they pray or walk by a Catholic church.

"Well how about this," Mr. Sekou said, handing each of the boys a sheet of paper and a pencil. "I want each of you to make a list of at least five things you really enjoy doing. Then, we will look over that list and see if we can make a career out of the things you listed."

"This is easy," Angel called out. "I love to sleep."

"And what kind of career or job could you get by sleeping?"

"He can be a professional dreamer because you said we should all have dreams," Myles joked. Everyone laughed. Everyone except for Mr. Sekou.

"Get serious, guys."

"I love to eat," Big Snacks called out, rubbing his big belly. They laughed again.

"Ha, Ha, Ha. Very funny, guys," Mr. Sekou mocked. "But seriously, you guys have to have a passion about something? Something that you really enjoy doing. Something that you wake up thinking about and go to sleep dreaming about. Once you find your passion, see if you can make money doing it. Then, before you know it, you will have a career."

Tafari sat in his chair, soaking in everything the animated Mr. Sekou had to say. It was the first time that Mr. Sekou commanded his attention. Come to think of it, it was the first time Mr. Sekou commanded the attention of the entire class. Before that day, Mr. Sekou delivered his day-to-day mini lessons in a very calm, laid back, monotone manner. But that day was different. When Mr. Sekou scanned the room, flames of passion sparkled in his eyes, veins pulsed in his neck when he spoke, and his neat locks swung back and forth when he snapped his head left and right, tossing insightful words into every corner of the classroom. It looked to Tafari as if Mr. Sekou had found his passion. Now, if only he and the boys that sat behind him could find theirs.

Chapter 14

As soon as the bell rang indicating the end of eigth period, Tafari hurried to the band room. He was the first to arrive and settled into the same seat as the day before. Big Snacks strolled in next with Myles walking closely behind. A short brown-skinned boy walked in, looking around like a tourist.

"You lookin' for Mr. Sekou?" Tafari called out.

"Yeah, I'm supposed to start the S.I.C.K. mentoring program today," the boy answered.

"He ain't get here yet," Tafari answered. "You might as well take a seat and get comfortable. We gonna be here for an hour." As the boy took a seat in the front, Tafari asked, "Yo, what's ya name, bruh?"

"Sha'King."

"Whatchu in here for, Sha'King?" Myles asked.

"My teacher wrote me up for video recording him on my phone."

"Why did you record him?" Tafari asked.

"Because he doesn't teach," Sha'King confessed.

"Really? I wanna be in *that* class," Big Snacks laughed.

"Me too," Myles joked.

"You say that now, but when you're failing the unit tests and state exams, I think you'll say different," Sha'King reasoned. "All Mr. Abraham does is give us these packets to do every day, and he never explains anything. Then when we're done with the packets, he just throws on a National Geographic video about sharks or seaweeds or something in the ocean. He never writes on the board and he rarely even speaks to us. It's like he doesn't even care."

"Ain't that the teacher that be selling candy to the students?" Tafari asked.

"Yeah, that's him," Sha'King answered. "When I'm sittin' in that class, not a minute goes by when someone isn't knockin' on the door. Right in the middle of class, while we're working on them stupid packets, he let's them in, opens his desk drawer, and lets the students pick whatever candy they want after he takes a dollar from them. I'm thinkin' about reporting him."

"Chill, chill!" Big Snacks exclaimed. "Don't do that! He's my backup plan whenever I can't find Biz."

"So, how did you get in trouble?" Tafari asked Sha'King.

"I pulled out my iPhone and video recorded him for fifteen straight minutes, sitting behind his laptop surfing the internet. He told me to shut my phone off and put it away but I told him I was gonna put it on YouTube and expose him as the worst teacher in the Bronx. He got upset and wrote me up for being defiant and refusing to put away my electronic device."

"Wow, maybe we should call you militant boy," Big Snacks joked.

"Look, I'm in school to learn and get an education. I'm not like most of these lazy students who just come to school to hang out and socialize. I wanna make something of my life."

It was at that time that Angel dragged in. "I can't believe I got almost two more weeks of this bull," he said, rolling his eyes as he looked around. "This is a waste of my time. I could be out in them streets makin' that money, know what 'm sayin'?"

"Yeah, I know whatchu mean," Myles replied.

"Yo, where that lame teacher at?" Angel asked.

"He ain't get here yet," Big Snacks answered. Angel took a seat in the back and began fiddling with the piano keys. Seconds of off-key noise soon turned into a soothing, familiar melody to Tafari's ears.

"Hey, that's a Tupac song," Tafari recognized.

"Yeah, 'I Ain't Mad Acha,'" Angel responded without lifting his eyes from the piano. Tafari, Big Snacks, Sha'King, and Myles stood beside Angel as he pounded the keys to the Tupac classic. Sha'King pulled out his iPhone and recorded Angel behind the piano.

"Check this out," Tafari said, clearing his throat. "I'ma spit a rhyme to that beat. Check it . . ."

Two ways outta the projects in cuffs or a casket

that's why rollin' up blunts is a habit

and thugs puff on that magic

to take their minds off crime any day you could take ya last breath

so watch ya step, before you walk into a bullet or stumble on ya death

there's gang wars goin' on outside my project window

I panic and think a bullet just whizzed by whenever I hear the wind blow

A friend of mine just got sent to the tomb

gone way too soon

only sixteen years removed from the womb.

Tafari paused in the middle of his rhyme because he felt a presence over his shoulder. "Mr. Sekou!" Tafari shrieked, as he turned around.

"Why did you stop?" Mr. Sekou asked, smiling like a proud dad. "It sounded real good."

"You think so?"

"Yeah. You sound like a young Nas."

"Who?"

"Nas. You don't know who Nas is?"

"I think I heard the name before."

"Nas is only the best lyricist ever in hip hop, next to Rakim."

"Is he one of them old school rappers?"

"No. Well, I guess he would be old school to you. But if you are serious about being a lyricist, I advise you to listen to some Nas. As a matter of fact, I got a copy of *Illmatic*, Nas's first album, in my bag. I never go anywhere without that CD. I'll give you a copy so you can listen to it."

"Cool."

"Are you going to listen to it?"

"I guess."

"I'm serious. I want you to listen to it carefully."

"Alright. I will listen to it only because you asked me to. It better be worth it."

"It will be. Trust me." Mr. Sekou turned to Angel. "And you got some skills on the piano. Where did you learn to play?"

"I taught myself. I just play by ear. If I hear it, then I can play it."

"When did you start listening to El Debarge?"

"Who?"

"That was an El Debarge song you was playing. It's called 'A Dream.'"

"Nah, Mr. Sekou," Big Snacks interrupted. "He was playin' a Tupac song."

"Well, Tupac and his producer used a sample from the El Debarge song. Either way, you got a lot of talent in those fingers, Angel."

"Thanks. But he's the one with the talent," Angel responded, pointing at Tafari. "Those lyrics were tight, man. I noticed you said what I said yesterday about there's only two ways outta the projects."

"Yeah," Tafari said. "I was inspired by that line. My mother used to say the same thing. I wrote it this morning in chemistry class."

"Yo, I'm cool wit' Kato Cash. You heard of him?"

"Heck yeah. Kato Cash is the hottest mixtape DJ on the streets."

"Well, I might be able to hook you up wit' him and we can do a song together."

"We?"

"Yeah, man. Me and Kato be makin' beats at his crib sometimes. He got this production program on his laptop that we be messin' around wit'."

"Let's do it."

"A'ight, I'll call him tonight and he'll set it up for us."

"Bet." Tafari and Angel slapped hands.

The next afternoon, after finishing up day three of Mr. Sekou's program, Tafari and Angel boarded a bus together and headed for Kato Cash's apartment. Fifteen minutes later, they arrived at Kato Cash's building and took the stairs to the third floor. A scrawny, shriveled-up Spanish lady with her head wrapped in a red scarf pulled the door open. She wrapped her wrinkled, pipe-cleaner arms around Angel's lower back and kissed him on the cheek. "How are you Angel? It's been so long."

"I'm good, Mrs. Acosta."

"How is your mom?"

"She's good."

"Tell her hola for me, okay?"

"I will," Angel said, turning to Tafari. "This is my friend, Tafari."

She smiled and nodded at Tafari and said, "Kato is in the back." Tafari waved at Mrs. Acosta as he followed Angel down the hall.

The first thing Tafari noticed when he entered Kato Cash's room was an audience of rappers and DJs. They were immortalized on stickers, posters, and CD covers that were plastered all over the eggshell-white walls. An old-looking keyboard sat lonely beneath the wall of fame on the left. Empty plastic cups and a paper plate of half-eaten Spanish rice and peas sat on top of the keys. A twin-sized bed was pushed up against the wall straight ahead. Dozens of CD cases were scattered across the blue bed sheets and even spilled to the nappy brown carpet.

Sitting to the right of the bed, in front of a computer monitor, was a chubby faced Puerto Rican guy with a pair of oversized headphones covering his ears. He swung around in his chair and looked up at Tafari through thin-rimmed glasses.

Tafari winced at Kato Cash's appearance. He couldn't believe the chubby computer geek that sat in front of him was the one responsible for putting out the hottest mix-tapes in the Bronx.

Angel spoke first. "Tafari, this is Kato Cash. Kato, this is Tafari, the dude I been tellin' you about."

"So Angel tells me that you're a lyrical genius," Kato said. "He says that you're the next hot rapper on the streets. Spit somethin' for me."

A wave of chills surfed up and down Tafari's back. The moment he had often daydreamed about was now a reality before him. Many nights, Tafari sat in front of his window, his rhyme book open in his left palm, pen in his right hand, eyes rolling back and forth over the blue lines of the page, lyrics on his tongue, ears open, listening to the inflections in his voice as he spit his rhymes to himself, and a big-time record executive on his mind. Kato Cash wasn't a record executive, but he was close enough. A step in the right direction. *If I spit some ill rhymes, I will be on my way*, Tafari thought.

Tafari's eyes were fidgety. They kept stumbling across the keyboard, and then the bed, and then Kato and his computer monitor, and then the keyboard again, and the bed again and Kato again. It took Tafari a minute to realize that his legs were fidgety too. He was pacing in circles in the room.

Tafari finally managed to stop pacing, but he couldn't keep his mind still. Over the months, Tafari had written enough rhymes to fill one hundred wastepaper baskets. He knew every single one of his rhymes by heart. Too bad there wasn't a place in his heart to store them.

His mind was all over the place, digging frantically for that one page of rhymes that he told himself was the best page of rhymes he had ever written. While his mind continued to dig, in its haste it knocked over every single one of those hundred wastepaper baskets at the same time. Hundreds of pages of rhymes scattered before his mind's eye like confetti. Tafari's mind's eye was able to snatch one line of rhymes from one page as it floated by, and another line of rhymes from another and fed them to his mouth.

Tafari stood in his b-boy stance and regurgitated the rhymes, one line at a time.

Believe the hype, I breathe life into trife thoughts

Um . . . and I'll put ya rap style on life support

And . . . um . . . my verbal glock will bang-bang

and make ya brains hang

. . . um . . . detroyin' rappers wit' rhymes that my mom says is strange slang

And . . . um . . ."

Kato Cash interrupted Tafari's choppy flow. "You a'ight. You a'ight . . . but um—"

"Yo, my bad for pausing in between rhymes, man," Tafari apologized. "It's just that . . . I can't even front. I'ma little nervous. Plus I'm havin' trouble rememberin' these rhymes . . . just give me a minute, let me sit down and collect my thoughts, and I'll definitely remember them."

"It's not even about you stoppin' and startin', homie," Kato said. "Like I said, your rhymes are alright. Yeah, you got some nice little punch lines, but you ain't sayin' nothin' that's real in the hood. You ain't sayin' nothin' that I could feel."

Shock froze Tafari in his b-boy stance. Nobody ever told Tafari that his rhymes were just *alright. What the heck did Kato Cash know about lyrics anyway?* Tafari thought. *He was just a DJ. A fake DJ at that. He ain't have any turntables. He ain't mix any records. All he did was get all the hottest songs at moment and burn them onto CDs and call them mixtapes. He ain't know anything about rhyming! And did I hear that chubby, speckled-face, buttoned-up-to-the-collar, plaid-shirt-wearing cornball say I wasn't saying nothing that was real in the hood? What the heck did he know about what was real in the hood? If I pulled my gun from my backpack and waved it in his speckled face, he'd probably use the bathroom all over his Fruit of the Looms.*

"Yo, Kato, man, I'm tellin' you, he's nice, just give him another chance," Angel pleaded. "Just let him spit somethin' else for you. I know he got somethin' you could feel."

Unable to get his thoughts straight, Tafari sat down, unzipped his backpack, and reached for his rhyme book. Tafari cursed under his breath when he couldn't find it. *I can't believe I left my rhyme book on my bed!* Tafari screamed in his head. *I just blew my big chance!* Just as Tafari was removing his hand from his backpack, he noticed his Bible tucked in between his binder and Algebra textbook.

Tafari was supposed to go straight to Bible study after leaving Mr. Sekou's class. But because of Kato Cash's hectic schedule, that afternoon was the only time that he and Tafari could meet. And Tafari wasn't about to blow his big chance. That is, until he left his rhyme book at home. Seeing the Bible reminded Tafari of the last time he left his rhyme book at home when he really needed it.

He was sitting in church when thoughts of the corner were circulating through his mind in rhyme form and he needed his rhyme book, immediately, so he could get what was in his head down on paper. Without his rhyme book, he became desperate, so he grabbed the Bible and searched for an empty page. He fished a pen from his pocket and lost himself as rhymes poured out of the ballpoint covering the inside cover of the Bible.

Tafari pulled the Bible from the backpack, stood up, and cleared his throat. "I'm ready."

"Ready for what? To preach?" Kato Cash joked.

"Nah. Ready to rhyme. Just listen." Tafari held the open Bible in front of his eyes and was ready to recite the scriptures. Not the holy scriptures, but the street scriptures. The ebonic-slang version of the scriptures written in rhyme form on the inside cover. Re-establishing his b-boy stance, Tafari cleared his throat and rhymed straight from the Bible.

I hang wit' endangered species

two Timberland-footed manimals who smoke the strangest weed-leaves and make their habitats on the corners of these mean streets

they're as real as it gets

they shoot hot slugs that'll barbecue ya rib tips

when their guns are sparkin'

it'll leak ya brains like Beef Lo Mein seapin' through the carton

they'll smoke you and whoever you standin' close to like charcoal

if you don't give up ya jewels pronto

they'll take ya goods, giddy-up and haul off like Tonto

don't resist, or bullets from their barrels will be screechin'

you'll be runnin', narrowly weavin'

you got hit and started bleedin'

but didn't know until you noticed ya apparel was leakin'

Now you needin' Doogie Howser treatment

marinatin' in ya own blood on the corner

wit' no signs of life in ya cornea

ya just another gonna, thugs spill a little beer

blow weed smoke in the air

in the hood, gangstas shed tattooed tears

these young villains have dead feelings, 'cause life is grim

when you die, another young street soldier is waitin' to step inside ya Timbs

and seek revenge, its homicidal cycle with no end.

Tafari's voice trailed off. Slowly, he lowered the Bible from his eyes. He peeked over at Kato Cash who remained still in his seat and wasn't showing any emotion on his face. With the back of his hand, Tafari wiped dried spittle from the corners of his mouth.

"I accidentally left my rhyme book at home," Tafari said, barely above a whisper. "But I didn't wanna waste ya time so I just spit this rhyme I wrote weeks ago. It's just some regular—"

"Yo, you got that rhyme outta the Bible?!" Kato Cash asked, springing to his feet. "Let me find out the prophets were spittin' rhymes in the Bible."

"Nah," Tafari laughed. "The rhyme just came to me one day and the only thing I had to write on was the Bible."

"I'm just messin' witchu," Kato Cash joked. "But seriously, that rhyme was hot, bruh! That's what I'm talkin' about! That's the type of rhyme that people in the streets need! I'm tired of the current state of hip hop where there's less focus on lyrics and more focus on third-grade-level hooks and casio beats! You gonna bring lyrics back!" Kato Cash was up out of his seat, his arms flaring from his body as he shouted. Kato Cash continued, "We gotta record that rhyme right now! You killed it! We gonna kill 'em in the streets when my new mixtape drops!"

"So, you're sayin' that you're gonna let me rhyme on ya new mixtape?"

"No doubt!" It took everything inside of Tafari to keep himself from squealing like a school girl.

"Yo, Kato, use the beat that me and you made the other day," Angel suggested.

"That's a good idea," Kato Cash agreed. He spun around in his seat, eyed the computer monitor and after a few clicks of the mouse, a loud beat boomed from the two speakers that stood under his computer desk. He reached up and started twisting the knobs of the racks that were stacked on top of each other on a shelf just above the computer monitor. Tafari was able to assume they were some kind of music production equipment.

"You think you can rhyme on that?" Kato Cash asked, nodding his head to the beat.

"No doubt," Tafari responded, confidently.

Kato Cash handed Tafari a pair headphones, not to put on his ears but to rhyme into because his microphone wasn't working. Tafari rhymed straight from the Bible, just like before. Except that time, he rhymed over a beat instead of acapella. Kato Cash told Tafari the mixtape would be a mix of exclusive songs from the current hottest rappers as well as special features from unsigned artists like Tafari. He also said the mixtapes would be available for download in a couple of days, and the CDs would hit the streets next week, but he gave Tafari a free advanced copy, with his verse and all. Angel remained at Kato's apartment, while Tafari left and took the bus back to the projects.

Tafari was bopping down the block, beaming like a kid on the last day of school as he clutched the brand new CD in his hand. A money-green wide-body Escalade swerved onto the block and screeched to a halt at the curb just in front of Tafari. Lil' Headache stuck his head out the passenger-side window. "What's good, Tafari?"

"Chillin'," Tafari shouted as he bopped to the passenger-side door and waved the CD in front of Lil' Headache's smile. "I just recoded a song on Kato Cash's new mixtape!" Tafari spouted, excitement soaked in his voice. "You gotta hear this, yo!"

"Word? Get in! Get in!" Tafari popped the door open and hopped in the back seat, next to Stretch and Los.

"Yo, Tafari, lemme introduce you to my homeboy," Lil' Headache said, pointing at the driver. "This is my boy, Trey Compton." A sinister, joker grin was etched just above Trey Compton's chin as he turned in his seat to greet Tafari. His face was the color of a vanilla wafer, and a black bandana was tied around his head like a headband, similar to the way Tupac Shakur used to wear his.

"What up, cuz?" Trey Compton greeted. "I been hearin' a lot aboutchu, homie. At some point, we need to sit down and break bread so we can talk business."

"What kind of business?" Tafari wondered.

"This ain't the time or place. Don't worry, we'll talk real soon." Trey Compton's brown eyes narrowed as he took a toke of the cigarette he held and blew smoke at Tafari before turning back around in his seat. Besides the smoke, the sudden tension in the air was thick enough to cut with a knife.

"Ain't this jeep fly, Tafari?" Lil' Headache asked, slicing into the tension.

"It is fly. Is this your jeep, Trey?" Tafari asked.

"Nah, its one of my chicks' father's jeeps. I gotta get it back before he gets home," Trey Compton responded. He and Lil' Headache shared a laugh.

"Gimme the CD so we can hear the song," Lil' Headache demanded. He took the CD and slid it in the CD player.

Tafari nodded, proudly, over the thumping bass while he sat on the plush leather seats.

"This song is heat!" Stretch called out over the bass. Still, Tafari only nodded. He didn't want to interrupt himself. Didn't want anyone in the jeep to miss any of his on-point lyrics that rattled out of the amps in the trunk.

Every single head in the jeep nodded in unison to the thumping bass of the beat. All of the windows in the jeep were down, allowing the beat to spill into the streets. "Is that you, Tafari?" one boy asked Tafari as he walked up to the passenger's side window. Tafari smiled and nodded, proudly. "It's bangin'!" the boy announced, before two-stepping up the street. Several girls had gathered on the curb and were dancing beside the jeep. A row of boys with their backs against the glass of the pizza shop were nodding their heads to the beat. *I can't believe that a song that I made is getting this type of reaction from the streets,* Tafari thought, sitting in awe as he took in the scenery.

Air hissing from the speakers snatched Tafari out of his thoughts. Trey Compton removed the CD and handed it back to Tafari. "The song is hot, homie," Trey Compton complimented.

"Thanks, man." Tafari put the CD in his jacket pocket as Los, Lil' Headache, and Stretch patted Tafari on the shoulder, complimenting him for his song. "Yo, I got some things I need to take care of," Tafari said, popping the door open and stepping onto the curb. "So, I'll catch up witchall later."

"Yeah, I'ma get out right here too," Stretch said. "Peace, y'all."

Tafari and Stretch stood on the curb as the jeep roared off and quickly descended down the hill.

"Yo, your song is flames, Tafari," Stretch said, slapping Tafari on the shoulder. "It's just a matter of time before you're the next big rapper. You on ya way, homie."

"Good lookin' out, man," Tafari thanked. "But, yo, whassup wit' Trey Compton? I didn't get a good vibe from him at all. Something about him made me a little uneasy."

"Yeah, I know whatchu mean," Stretch agreed. "Ever since he got here, he's made me feel a little uneasy, too. That's why I got outta the jeep."

"Where did he come from?"

"He's from Compton, California, and he just moved over here about a week ago. I think he's living with his aunt or somethin'."

"*Compton?!*" Tafari shouted. "I knew that name sounded familiar. That's where Easy-E and Dr. Dre are from. That's were them real gangbangers live."

"Yeah, it ain't hard to tell that Trey was involved in gangs out there. As a matter of fact, he got us operating like a real gang now."

"Whatchu mean?"

"He made all of us wear black flags," Stretch removed the black bandana from his back pocket. "He said the flags will identify who is down wit' us and who is not. He also gave us a name. We're officially NSG, short for the North Side Gang. And get this—Trey Compton has made himself the general of the crew. And he named Headache as his right hand man."

"What about me?"

"I don't know." Stretch shrugged. "What I do know is, every time I brought up your name and talked about you, Trey Compton would get agitated and upset. It was almost like he was jealous of you. It was clear to me from day one that the moment he showed up, he wanted to take over. I think that's what he meant when he said y'all needed to talk business."

"It all makes sense now," Tafari said. "In order for him to officially be the general, I have to go."

"Or agree to just be one of the guys."

"One of the guys?" Tafari huffed. "I ain't about to let no out-of-town dude come over here and take over my block. I earned my stripes. I shot Dready, remember?"

"Of course I remember," Stretch said. "So, are you sayin' you gonna go to war with Trey Compton?"

"N-no," Tafari hesitated. "I don't know what I'm sayin'. I have a lot on my mind right now. I'm outta here. I'll see you around, Stretch." They gave each other dap and a half hug and both went their separate ways.

Chapter 15

Mr. Sekou's head nodded furiously while listening to Tafari's song on the portable CD player that sat on the teacher's desk. Though his head reacted to the beat, Mr. Sekou's face reacted to the lyrics, grimacing at the vivid imagery and smiling at the punch lines.

"This is pretty good," Mr. Sekou announced as the song ended. "You have a lot of talent, Tafari."

"What about me?" Angel called out from his seat in the back. "I helped make the song too."

"What did you do?"

"I played the piano part of the beat."

"It takes a lot of talent to play the piano the way you played it. You could be the next Stevie Wonder."

"Who?"

"Stevie Wonder! One of the greatest musicians ever! He made songs like 'Master Blaster', 'Superstition', 'Living for the City', and 'Isn't She Lovely.' Do any of those songs ring a bell?" Mr. Sekou was greeted by blank stares from the boys. "He's blind, he has long braids, and he also made a song called 'I Just Called to Say I Love You.'"

"I know that song!" Sha'King called out. "My mom calls me and my brother Young Marcus at random times and sings that to me."

"I ain't tryna make no records like 'I Just Called to Say I Love You' and soft stuff like that," Angel complained. "That's old. I'm tryna make some new heat. Somethin' gangsta that'll be hot in the streets today."

"And you can," Mr. Sekou said. "But you need a plan. You have to map out a plan and figure out how you can become the big-time producer you want to be. Living day by day and running around in the streets with a 'forget tomorrow' attitude ain't going to cut it."

"What about me?" Big Snacks asked. "What kind of job could I get in the future?"

"Well, you said you love to eat," Mr. Sekou began. "You could be a professional food critic."

"What's that?"

"A food critic gets paid to taste food from different restaurants all around the world and then you get to critique it in an article or blog."

"Wait a minute," Big Snacks said, standing up out of his seat, salivating. "You mean to tell me I can get a job where I'm paid to eat? Sign me up, right now!" Everyone laughed.

"Do you ever cook, Big Snacks?"

"Yeah, when I'm hungry and there ain't nothin' to eat."

"Is it good?"

"Heck yeah. I remember this one time when I got home from school and I was starvin'. We had a couple of pieces of left over chicken legs and a little bit of left-over stuffing in the fridge but it wasn't enough for me, my mom, and my two little sisters. So I cut the chicken into pieces, put it in a bowl, and combined it with the stuffing. I remembered my mom always said that I don't eat enough vegetables, so I found a pack of frozen broccoli in the freezer and added it with the chicken and stuffing. I added some diced onions, some shredded cheddar cheese, an egg, some milk, some butter, salt, and pepper. I poured it into a casserole pan and just by looking at it, I knew it needed a crust on top. One of my sisters had half of a bag of butter crackers in her lunch box. I crumbled it and spread over the casserole and put it in the oven for forty-five minutes. When my mom got home from work, she was so proud of me for making dinner. Man, I tell ya, that chicken and broccoli casserole was better than anything my mama ever made. Just don't tell her I said that."

"So, you were improvising, like a real chef. Ever thought about being a chef?"

"No, not really."

"Well, there's another option for you," Mr. Sekou pointed out. "Like I said the other day, just find your passion, and then see if you can make a career out of it."

"My passion is girls," Myles admitted, silly smirk on his lips.

"I know what kind of job you can get, but I don't think it's legal," Big Snacks joked. Laughter erupted in the band room.

"There are plenty of things you can do. You could be a relationship expert where you give guys dating tips—"

"He can't be a relationship expert," Angel cut in. "How he goin' give datin' tips when I seen so many girls dis that fake playa."

"You lyin' through ya crooked, yellow teeth," Myles spat. "You ain't never see me get rejected by a girl."

"Yo, you better watch who you talkin' to like that," Angel threatened, standing up out of his seat.

"Chill out!" Mr. Sekou yelled, stepping between Myles and Angel. "We ain't having that in here today. Now, listen up. I have a group activity for you guys that I think will be fun. This exercise is called 'Johari's Window' and it's desgined to help you understand your relationship with yourself and others."

"Relationship with ourselves?" Myles asked.

"Don't act like you don't be relatin' to ya self when you be in ya room, alone," Big Snacks cracked. The boys howled with laughter.

"Yo, forget you, fat boy!" Myles shot back.

"Alright, guys, let's get serious," Mr. Sekou said, slicing through the laughter. "I need each of you to grab a desk and push it to the center of the room and form a circle." After the boys positioned the desks as Mr. Sekou instructed, each of them took a seat and was handed a blank piece of paper, a pack of sticky notes, and a pen.

"Draw a big, square on the paper that I gave you," Mr. Sekou announced. "Next, divide the square into four boxes. In the first box, write 'known self' and in the second box write 'façade.'" Mr. Sekou paused and walked around the circle of chairs to make sure everyone was doing as instructed. "Now, in the third box write 'blind spot' and in the fourth box, write 'unknown.'" Mr. Sekou paused again and waited. After helping Angel and Big Snacks spell façade, and informing Myles that the second box should be beneath the first box, not across from it, Mr. Sekou handed each of the boys a sheet of paper with fifty–seven adjectives printed on it.

"Alright, here's the first step. In the first box where you wrote 'known self,' pick three to four adjectives that decribe you. Write the adjectives on the sticky notes and stick them on the first box. The 'known self' box is what you know about yourself and it's what your peers know about you, as well." Mr. Sekou monitored the group as the boys picked adjectives and wrote them on sticky notes.

"Anyone want to share?" Mr. Sekou asked.

"I'll share," Sha'King said, hand in the air.

"The floor is yours, Sha'King."

"Alright, so, the adjectives that describe me are: intelligent, confident, ingenious, knowledgeable, helpful, self-assertive—"

"Yo, what's the matter witchu, man?" Angel interrupted. "Three or four adjectives, that's it! Why you tryna put all fifty-seven adjectives in one box?"

"I can't help it if I found more than four adjectives that describe me," Sha'King shot back, leaning over to get glimpse of Angel's paper. "And how you tryna tell me the rules when you ain't following them yaself. You only got one word in ya box." Angel glared at Sha'King.

"What adjective did you pick for your 'known self' box, Angel?" Mr. Sekou asked.

"I wrote the word 'gangsta.'"

"'Gangsta' ain't on the list," Sha'King pointed out.

"I know it ain't," Angel stated. "But *gangsta* describes me perfect and everybody knows it."

"Yo, Mr. Sekou?" Myles stood up. "How you gon' let Angel pick a word that ain't on the list? That ain't fair."

"Why don't you mind ya business!?" Angel stood up.

"Why don't you make me?" Myles shot back.

"Alright, guys, calm down!" Mr. Sekou shouted, stepping between the boys. "Myles and Angel, sit down, now!" Mr. Sekou waited for both boys to sit before he continued. "If any one of ya'll use a word that's not on the list, it's okay because this is our first time trying this exercise. Besides, there might be some adjectives on the list that you do not know the meaning to—"

"I know the meanings of all the adjectives on this list," Sha'King cut in. "I'm always reading and—"

"Of course you know the meaning of all the words because you're a nerd," Angel laughed.

"I ain't no nerd, homie," Sha'King snapped. "Ain't nothing awkward or socially inept about me. I am an intelligent, young, black teen that reads a lot because I seek knowledge and truth. But at this point, I'll be more than happy to stoop to your level and whip ya ignorant—"

"Guys! Guys! Guys!" Mr. Sekou yelled, veins pulsing from his neck. "Enough is enough, already! Now, everyone be quiet, and let's finish this activity and have some fun." Mr. Sekou waited for Sha'King and Angel to sit, before he continued. "Alright, let's move on to a different box," Mr. Sekou announced. "Let's go to the box marked 'blind spot.' In this box, the adjectives are selected only by the peers. This is what our peers know about us that we don't know about ourselves. In order to complete this box, we need to partner up. So, I'm going to need Myles and Big Snacks to partner up; Angel and Tafari, you two partner up; and, Sha'King, I'll be your partner."

"I still don't get the 'blind spot' box," Big Snacks admitted.

"I can explain it to him," Tafari volunteered. "Basically, it's like this. Take Angel for example. In the 'known self' box, he wrote 'gangsta' because that's how he sees himself. In the 'blind spot' box, we write how we see him. And the way we see him might be way different than how he sees himself."

"No, it ain't," Big Snacks said. "I see him the same way he sees himself. He's gangsta." Angel smiled proudly.

"I don't see him as *gangsta*," Tafari disagreed. "If I had to pick an adjective for Angel's 'blind spot,' I would pick 'caring.'"

"Lemme find out *gangsta Angel* is caring," Myles joked.

"Angel, the Care Bear Gangsta," Sha'King laughed.

"Yo, ya'll tryna play me like I'm soft or somethin'!" Angel shouted, standing up and eyeballing Tafari.

"I only say caring because you barely know me, yet, you still introduced me to Kato Cash to fulfill a dream of mine," Tafari said, defending his choice.

"I ain't tryna hear all that!" Angel snapped, waving his hands in Tafari's face. "I represent them Southside Boys, know what 'm sayin'? Calling me names can get you jumped on sight."

"Southside!" Myles shouted back. "You from the southside?"

"All day!" Angel proclaimed, thumping his chest with a closed fist.

"I wouldn't say that so loud if I were you. My boy Tafari represents the northside."

"You from the *soft*side?!" Angel shouted at Tafari, eyes slit in anger. "I don't like the *soft*side. Dudes from the *soft*side jumped my cousin and robbed him. Plus, some dude over there shot my homie in the leg. I think his name was

. . ." Angel's words trailed off and his eyes widened as if he finally put two and two together. ". . . Tafari! I knew ya name sounded familiar. You the one that shot my homeboy!" Angel charged at Tafari like an outside linebacker. Big Snacks stepped in between the two and body blocked Angel like an offensive lineman, just before he reached Tafari. Mr. Sekou grabbed Tafari by the arm and pulled him toward the front of the room, shielding him from Angel's attack. "What's going on here?!" Mr. Sekou shouted. "Everybody sit down so we can talk about this!"

"I can't sit in the same room wit' that dude!" Angel bellowed, still trying to wiggle free from Big Snacks's grip.

"You mean to tell me just because y'all live on opposite sides of the projects, ya'll can't get along?"

Tafari shook his head. "No, we can't," Angel agreed.

"But you guys just did a song together," Mr. Sekou reasoned. "Y'all talked about making an album together and now y'all wanna kill each other because of some stupid gangs?"

"If I woulda known he was from the northside, I would have never taken him to meet Kato Cash," Angel grunted.

"And I would have never went witchu," Tafari shot back.

"Let me tell y'all something," Mr. Sekou said, stepping between Angel and Tafari. "Gangs are for cowards who are afraid to fend for themselves and stand up on their own two feet. Most of these gang members are too scared or too ignorant to realize how powerful they can be. We just talked about how much talent is in this room. We got a future chef in this room. A future rap artist or songwriter or writer of the next great novel is in this room. A future music producer or music writer or designer of the next innovative production program is in this room. But you guys just want to throw it all away so you can kill each other over streets and blocks that you don't own."

"Man, you don't even know whatchu talkin' 'bout," Angel snapped. "You just a lame teacher. You don't know nothin' 'bout these streets."

"Is that what you really think?" Mr. Sekou challenged.

"Only thing you know about are them outdated textbooks." Mr. Sekou unbuttoned his cuffs and rolled up both of his sleeves. He placed his bare forearms together, palms up, as the boys gathered in to get a closer look. "Would a lame teacher who didn't know about the streets have tats like these?" Mr. Sekou asked sarcastically. The boys examined the dark tattoos imprinted on his forearms. "Gun Hill!" Myles exclaimed. "It's crazy over there. Is that where you're from?"

"Born and raised," Mr. Sekou stated. "Gun Hill wasn't, and still to this day, ain't no joke. Don't get it twisted: I'm educated now, but twenty years ago, I was 'bout that life. Guns, drugs, you name it."

"So then you know what it's like to be a teenager from the projects. So why you trippin'?" Angel asked.

"You're the one that's trippin' for not listening to what I have to say," Mr. Sekou began. "The difference between me and you is I didn't have anyone who had already been through the struggle to school me. I didn't have any adults or mentors that I respected to pull me aside and show me that there was more than two ways out of the projects." Mr. Sekou paused and put his finger to his temple. "Your mind, your imagination, is the way out. I had to find that out the hard way. Nearly lost my life in the process, but I survived, and I'm still here. A lot of my friends didn't make it. I've been to more prison visiting rooms and funeral parlors than I can count. I can help you guys avoid the same traps that me and my friends fell victim to. Tafari, Angel, it ain't cool dying or going to jail before you turn eighteen and making your mommas cry. It's cool to live to a hundred, raise kids that'll be productive citizens in the world, and make your mommas proud. This is all possible, just let me help you."

"I'm definitely gonna make that punk's momma cry before he makes my momma cry!" Angel shouted at Tafari. He juked one way and spun around Big Snacks like a slick running back. Mr. Sekou, the last line of defense, caught Angel just before he reached Tafari.

"Okay, class is over for today," Mr. Sekou announced as he carried Angel outside of the classroom. "Big Snacks, Myles, make sure he leaves the building," Mr. Sekou ordered. "I wanna stay behind and talk to Tafari." Big Snacks and Myles nodded and exited the classroom. "I'll get security," Sha'King offered. Mr. Sekou locked the classroom door after they left. He took a seat beside Tafari.

"Tafari, I've wanted to have a one-on-one discussion with you for a while now," Mr. Sekou said, taking a seat at the desk beside Tafari.

"About what?" Tafari asked.

"I've noticed a big change in you over the last month or so."

"What kind of change?"

"For example, your attire changed," Mr. Sekou began. "At the beginning of the school year, you used to come to school in khakis, button-up shirts, and shoes with rubber soles. About a month ago, you started coming to class in Timberlands and hoodies."

"Ain't nothin' unusual about that," Tafari tried to reason. "Fashion trends change almost every week. And hey, I'ma teenager; I gotta keep up with the latest trends in order to fit in, right?"

"You weren't too concerned with keeping up with the latest trends until about a month ago," Mr. Sekou said. "And it was about a month ago when I started seeing you hanging out with the wrong crowd."

"You stalkin' me, now?"

"No, not at all," Mr. Sekou laughed. "But it wasn't until recently that I started seeing you hanging out with Alphonso Naismith, Carlos Delgado, and Damian Robinson. That's around the same time your clothes, your demeanor, and your school habits changed."

"What do you mean, my school habits changed?"

"Well, I looked through your school records, and you've never, ever cut class before. That is, until a month ago. Did you know you cut a total of seven classes this month?" Tafari shrugged and eyed the floor. Mr. Sekou continued, "I matched up the days and times you cut class with the days and time that Alphonso, Damian, and Carlos cut class and guess what? It's a perfect match. So what's up, Tafari? What's going on? Why the sudden change?" Tafari studied the stained, tiled floor as if the answer he needed was written down there. His mind developed what he thought was a reasonable excuse that he was going to give to Mr. Sekou until he lifted his eyes and they brushed over Mr. Sekou's tattoos. The markings on his forearms were about as cluttered and colorful as the arms of the OGs he had seen roaming the streets and the stern look in Mr. Sekou's penetrating eyes was more intimidating than some of the glares he tried to avoid on the corners of the roughest avenues. *If there is any teacher in the world that would understand what I'm going through, it's Mr. Sekou,* Tafari thought.

He inhaled slowly through his nostrils and exhaled his words. "It all started when I got jumped on the south-side after walking my ex-girlfriend to her building. That's when I knew that a northside dude like me had no business being on the southside. Then, a few days later, I'm on the train and another southside dude puts a gun to my face and forces me to strip off my clothes. He didn't know I was from the northside, but my outfit was similar to the one I wore when I got jumped. It became clear to me that the outfits I was wearing, my shoes, my khakis, and my ties were like a billboard that read 'sucker.' So, I figured if I dressed like the thugs that hung out around my way, I wouldn't be a target anymore. I just wanted to blend in. I never wanted to be a part of a gang. It just kind of happened."

"Why did Angel say that you shot someone? Is this true?"

"It was an accident," Tafari pleaded. "I didn't mean to do it. He put the gun to my face and I tried to wrestle it from him and the gun just went off and he got hit in the leg."

"You don't have to tell me if you want to, but do I know the guy that got shot in the leg?"

"I don't mind tellin' you," Tafari shrugged. "It was Dready."

"So, you're the one that shot Kenroy Davis," Mr. Sekou stated with a raised eyebrow. "I heard that he had gotten shot, but never would have suspected you. But, as for Dready, I know him very well. He's a very troubled young man."

"I'm just glad he's overseas in Jamaica and I don't have to see him ever again," Tafari admitted.

"Overseas? Who told you that?" Mr. Sekou asked.

"I heard—"

"You heard wrong," Mr. Sekou interrupted. "The only Jamaica Dready been to is Jamaica, Queens."

"But no one has seen him in weeks," Tafari said.

"That's because he's been hiding out at his grand-mother's house in Queens while his leg and ego heal. Mr. Sullivan has spoken with his mom and he should be coming back to school any day now." Tafari's stomach nearly swallowed itself and came back up out of his mouth when he thought about running into Dready again. He should have known better than to believe the projects' rumors that Dready fled the country.

"Wow! You just caught me off guard with the news of Dready coming back. I didn't think I would see him again."

"Look, I'll make sure he doesn't come near you when you're here at school."

"I'm not worried about bumping into him in school. I'm more worried about bumping into him outside of school. But, I'll be a'ight. I'll have my crew with me."

"Speaking of your crew," Mr. Sekou said, shifting his position on the hard chair. "I really think you should consider cutting them off."

"Why?"

"Look, I know I can't tell you who to be friends with, but they will hold you back from your dreams. I've tried to reach Damian—I mean, Lil' Headache—plenty of times and I have to say, he's about as unreachable as any student I've come across. I know I'm not supposed to say that as a teacher, but I'm just trying to be real with you right now, Tafari. Los is a follower, and just like Lil' Headache, he is almost at the point of no return. But you're different. I can hear it in your music. I never told anybody this, but when I was your age, I wanted to be an emcee too."

"You, a rapper? I can't picture it," Tafari chuckled.

"Believe it or not, I was pretty good with the rhymes. But when I was your age, I was nowhere near as good as you are, Tafari."

"Fareal?"

"Fareal. Even now, at the age of thirty-something, I couldn't dream of writing like you. You're a very skilled writer. Your lyrics are very insightful and deep. I can see it in your eyes. There's hope in them. I can't say that about your friend's eyes, except for Alphonso. I've been trying to help him stay out of trouble and focus on his passion."

"Basketball?"

"Yes. I've been at the school for eight years and he's the best basketball player I have ever seen at this school. Coach Holloway says the same thing. But just like you, he's a prisoner to peer pressure. He's trying to fit in, just like you were when you changed your wardrobe. But from being around you these past couple of days, I can tell that you're not a street dude. You're intelligent, thoughtful, sympathetic, trustworthy—all the adjectives that you don't normally use to describe a street dude."

"Are those all the adjectives that you would place in my 'blind spot' box?" Tafari joked.

"Yes, that's how I see you. You probably didn't have any idea that someone sees you as intelligent, thoughtful, sympathetic, and trustworthy, did you?"

"No, except for the intelligent part," Tafari laughed.

"Tafari, you're a very talented writer with a good heart and bright future. But that future won't be possible if you continue to hang around with that crew on the streets."

"I can't stop hangin' wit my crew *just like that.*"

"Why not?"

"Because I got my rep to protect," Tafari retorted. "If I stop hangin' wit' my boys, they gonna think I'ma sucka or something."

"Your *rep*?" Mr. Sekou repeated.

"Yeah, you know, my reputation."

"I know what *rep* means."

"So you know that a rep is all you have when you're on the streets."

"Yeah, I know all about having a rep," Mr. Sekou confessed. "When I was your age, running around on the streets, two of my best friends were more concerned about their street reps than anything else. Do you know where they are now?"

"Where?"

"Buried next to each other at Woodlawn Cemetery." Tafari bowed his head and eyed his boots as Mr. Sekou continued. "Tafari, you have to understand the bigger the rep you have on the streets, the bigger the target is on your back. I don't care how tough you think you are, there is always someone on the streets that's tougher. And if you're the one with the biggest rep, then you better believe a lot of street dudes are going to come after you."

"Come after me for what?"

"To rob you, jump you, or to kill you. What better way for a street dude to get themselves a rep than to do something to you? You are the teenager with one of the biggest reps, right?"

"The streets are a lot more complicated than I thought it was," Tafari revealed. "I was better off when I watched the streets from my window and I was still wearing my slacks and button-up shirts. At least *that* target was smaller."

"Tafari, you gonna have to choose. What's more important to you, your *rep* or your life?" Mr. Sekou's question was a slap upside the head. Deep down, Tafari knew Mr. Sekou was right, but how could he face his boys and tell them that he didn't want to hang with them anymore? What would happen to his reputation if he stopped hanging on the corner?

Chapter 16

It was 3:20 p.m. when Mr. Sekou dismissed Tafari. As soon as Tafari exited through the back entrance of the school, he called Malikah on her cell.

"Malikah, I wanna see you. Where are you?"

"See me when?"

"Now."

"Now? It's twenty minutes after three. Ain'tchu supposed to be at that afterschool program right now?"

"Yeah, but we got out early today. So where are you?"

"I . . . um . . ."

"Who is that I hear in the background?"

"What? Whatchu talkin' 'bout?"

"I hear someone in the background."

"You trippin'. Ain't nobody in the background."

"I just heard a dude's voice."

"Maybe you're hearing the TV because I'm at home."

"If you're at home why do I hear honking car horns?"

"What?!"

"You heard me. It sounds like you are in the streets right now."

"Um . . . I gotta go. I'll talk to you later." *Click.*

I can't believe she just hung up on me, Tafari said to himself. Tafari put his cell phone away but the baritone voice in the background as Malikah spoke, as well as the car horns and other familiar project noises, was still playing in the back of his mind. Tafari chased the familiar echoes in the back of his head to a place where he knew he heard them before.

Tafari raced to the block where he and his crew usually hung. He poked his head in the pizza shop and Lee's Kitchen, scanning the faces of the patrons in search of Malikah. Looking up and down the block, Tafari spotted Malikah on the curb opening the passenger door to a gold Acura.

"Malikah!" Tafari called out. As Malikah turned in the direction of the voice, shock froze her in her stance as if it was the ghost of Tafari that had shouted her name. Tafari wore a smug "you're busted" smirk as he approached. "I thought you were at home!" Tafari snapped. "Why did you lie to me?"

"I lied because I didn't wanna hurt you."

"Too late!" Tafari erupted. "I can't believe you cheatin' on me!" Tafari stormed to the passenger's side window, bent over at the waist to get a look at the dude who would dare try to mess with his girl. Tafari's face was wrinkled with anger as the dark tinted window sank, slowly. Tafari was nearly blinded by the glare of the sincere golden smile of the driver. The driver's gold fronts weren't the only thing shining in the car. A glint of light beaming from the silver pistol sticking out of the waistband of the driver's jeans attracted Tafari's eyes. The sight of the iron in the driver's waist smoothed out the creases of anger in Tafari's face, instantly. The gun, the car, the gold teeth, the chunky gold watch, and matching gold chain appealed to Tafari's better senses and told him that the driver was a drug dealer. Tafari knew to back off.

"What did I ever do to you to deserve this?" Tafari asked, turning to Malikah.

"Deserve what?" Malikah shot back. "All I'm doing is going to get something to eat."

"I can take you to get something to eat. Come on, I'll buy you a pizza."

"I'm tired of pizza. That's all you ever buy for me."

"Alright, then I'll buy you some Chinese food. Let's go."

"I don't want Chinese food either. I'm sick of eating on this block all the time. I wanna be taken out and wined and dined. Botchy offered to take me to Red Lobster and I accepted."

"I can take you to Red Lobster."

"How? You ain't got no car."

"We can take the bus."

"The bus? Me, on the bus? I don't think so."

"Since when were you too good to ride the bus?"

"Since I got guys offering me free rides in nice cars."

"How about if I call a cab to take us there and then I can buy you Red Lobster."

"Do you have Red Lobster money?"

"Not right now, but I can get it by next week."

"Next week? I'm hungry right now."

"So you're gonna cheat on me because I can't afford Red Lobster?" Tafari asked. "If you really love me, you supposed to *ride or die* with me even if I'm broke."

"But you're always broke," Malikah stated matter-of-factly.

"Let me ask you something. Somebody told me they be seeing you in the school hallway and on the street walking with different guys all the time. Is this true?"

"What's wrong with me having male friends?"

"People around here know you my girl. But if they see you wit' another dude, it makes me look like a lame. You gonna have people talkin' behind my back and . . . it just looks bad."

"I'm not tryna make you look bad but I can't help it if a lot of guys are attracted to me because I'm beautiful. I been turnin' down dudes left and right for you, and I'll tell you, it's gettin' harder and harder, especially when they offer to buy me stuff. I got dude's offering to take me to the movies and wanting to buy me jewelry. I've decided I'm not going to turn them down anymore."

"So, it's like that now. Any guy that offers to buy you a ring or take you to a fancy restaurant, you're just gonna accept it and ignore my feelings?"

"You don't understand, Tafari. You don't know what I go through. It's really hard for me."

"Hey, where's the ring I bought for you?" Tafari asked, glaring at Malikah's blank ring finger.

"Oh—um . . . it got stolen."

"Stolen? By who?"

"It was—" Botchy tooted the car horn, provoking Malikah to open the passenger side door. "Call me later or something. I gotta go." Malikah took a seat in the car and slammed the door shut. Tafari stood, helpless, as the gold Acura screeched away from the curb and descended down the hill. "Yo, Tafari!" a familiar voice called out. Tafari turned around and cracked a half smile at Stretch as he approached. They gave each other dap and a half hug.

"You a'ight man?" Stretch asked. "You look like someone just stole something from you."

"I did have something stolen. My girl."

"Whatchu talkin' about?"

"Malikah just jumped into the car of a drug dealer and they drove off to Red Lobster, right in my face. I just stood here and did nothing about it. I feel like a punk right now. I should have done something."

"Like what, get yaself killed?" Stretch asked. "You said he was a drug dealer. I'm pretty sure he had a gun on him."

"Yeah, he did have a gun. I saw it."

"It was smart not to try anything, especially for Malikah. Let's be real, Malikah is fly and all, but did you really think she was gonna be faithful to you? I don't know if you know this, but when Malikah first moved around here at the beginning of the school year, all the dudes on the block was tryna get wit' her. But this hustler called Green-Eyes had more clout than anyone around here and he bagged her first. About a month later he gets arrested and then she starts talkin' to Dready. Then, right after you shot Dready, she left him and came to you. You think she would have gotten witchu if you didn't shoot Dready and get the rep that you have now?"

"Probably not."

"Exactly. Now some drug dealer wit' a bigger rep than you wants to get wit' her and she leaves you for him. And I bet you if a bigger drug dealer with more money tries to get with her next week, she'll leave the dude she just went to Red Lobster with for him."

"I know you're right but it still hurts, man."

"Man, you'll get over her. There are plenty of good lookin' girls around the way."

"Yeah, but none as fly as Malikah."

"True."

"Stretch, what happened to your eye?" Tafari asked, as he lifted his sad eyes from the concrete and looked at Stretch for the first time since they started conversing. He noticed a purple blood clot in his right eye and puffiness just below his right eye lid.

"I got jumped," Stretch replied.

"Jumped by who?"

"Trey Compton, Lil' Headache, and Los."

"Why did they jump you?"

"In order to be officially down with NSG, you gotta get jumped in. That's the new rule that Trey Compton added."

"But you were already down."

"Actually, I wasn't," Stretch revealed. "It's like Trey Compton hit the reset button. Everything started over when he arrived on the scene."

"So, everyone had to get jumped in?"

"Everyone except him and Lil' Headache."

"What? That's crazy."

"They been jumpin' people in, left and right. We're like eight deep now. Just earlier, they jumped in some dude name PK who wanted to be down."

"PK?!" Tafari shrieked. "Is he a short, stocky dude?"

"Yeah, you know him?"

"Yeah. He's the youth pastor at the church by C Town."

"A youth pastor turned gangsta?"

"Yup."

"Wow, that's crazy."

"I know."

"Anyway, now it's your turn to get jumped in."

"Me!" Tafari shrieked. "Wait a minute. How does a foreigner come to our block and take over everything? What does Headache have to say about this?"

"You know how Headache is," Stretch explained. "He is in awe of gangsters. Don't get me wrong, Headache *gets it in*. He can fight and he'll rob you blind. But he ain't never been no real gangsta. He ain't never bust no gun. That's why he admired you so much because not only did you stand up to Dready, but you shot him. Headache used to brag about you all the time. But ever since Trey Compton arrived—"

"He forgot all about me," Tafari cut in.

"Pretty much. Headache is like a little puppy dog around Trey, following him around, begging him to tell him gangsta stories from Compton."

"So why didn't Headache have to get jumped in?"

"Because like I told you before, Trey named himself the general and Headache his right hand man. Only the soldiers get jumped in."

"So I'm just a soldier now?"

"According to Trey Compton, yeah."

"Stretch, let me ask you somethin'," Tafari said, changing the subject. "You ever thought about leavin' this street stuff behind and focusing on your dreams?"

"Dreams? I ain't got no dreams."

"You ain't never had dreams about playin' in the NBA.?"

"People from around here don't make it to the NBA."

"Plenty of players made it outta the projects and got drafted."

"Like who?"

"LeBron James and Allen Iverson."

"Sometimes I be thinkin' those stories are fake, like some made-for-TV drama. How come I ain't never seen them around here?"

"Look, Mr. Sekou even said that you're the most talented basketball player he ever seen at the school."

"Mr. Sekou is nosy and needs to mind his business. He always thinks he can solve everyone's problems like he got all the answers."

"Well, he helped me. I been thinkin' about leavin' these streets alone, man."

"Why?"

"I been havin' these weird dreams lately, man."

"What kind of dreams?"

"I'm on the corner, right over there." Tafari pointed at the deli just a few stores down. "And all of a sudden, water just comes at me from all angles and surrounds me. I'm splashin' around 'cause I can't swim and I reach for my gun which looks like a floating device and it just deflates or dissolves in my hand. Then, I see my rhyme book and it looks like a branch. But it's just out of reach. Just before I drown, I reach out for the book and then I wake up. I've had this same dream about three times but I don't know what it means."

"I'm not a dream analyst," Stretch explained. "But I think it's a sign that you should focus on your music and probably leave this street stuff alone."

"You think so?"

"Yeah, man. You're nice wit' the rhymes. You gotta better chance of gettin' a deal than I do of gettin' drafted."

"I don't know about that. You're amazin' on the basketball court."

"Thanks, man."

"How tall are you, Stretch?"

"When I got my physical last summer, the doctor said that I was six-foot-three and still growing."

"Wow! You should really think about focusing on basketball. You even said it yaself, you're not gettin' good vibes from Trey Compton. The way he's changin' things around, it's about to get *real* on these streets."

"You can say that again," Stretch agreed.

"I'm torn, Stretch," Tafari disclosed. "A part of me doesn't want to turn my back on the streets because I don't want anybody thinking I'ma punk and I'm running from Trey Compton. Then, the other side of me wants to leave these crazy streets alone to focus on my music. I got a lot to think about."

"Well, while you're thinkin' about it, you better watch your back 'cause they're lookin' for you."

"What if I tell them I don't want to be down anymore?"

"Then, they are probably still gonna jump you, because you also gotta get jumped out."

"But that doesn't make any sense," Tafari said, scratching the side of his head. "How they gonna jump me in to a gang that I'm not technically in, but at the same time jump me out if I was never jumped in in the first place?"

"Nothing makes sense anymore." Stretch shrugged. "Just be on the look out."

"I will."

"Peace, man."

After Stretch walked off, Tafari ran home and dashed into his room to get his gun. While standing in the middle of his room with the handle of the thrity-eight in his grip, Tafari turned and caught a glimpse of his reflection in his window. A face from Tafari's past appeared in the glass. The reflection's guiltless eyes were staring back into Tafari's, studying his face as if he didn't recognize him. Tafari recognized the face in the glass instantly. It was the face he used to wear about a month ago when he sat safely behind his window on the radiator, wishing to be apart of the noise the thugs were making outside. After meeting his new crew, Tafari changed faces with the mad-face thug that often hid behind his eyes. It was almost as if Tafari flipped himself inside out; the hidden thug was now on the outside and his known self was buried deep inside where no thug on the outside of his window could detect it.

That face represented a time when it was "all so simple," like that Wu-Tang song Mr. Sekou was listening to one day in the classroom, Tafari thought.

Tafari left his old face behind in the window glass, and his gun in the boot box under his bed. He left his apartment and walked aimlessly down the block. His head hung low, heavy with the words of Mr. Sekou's conversation from earlier. Tafari was supposed to be going to Bible study for the first time in weeks, but his mind was too bogged down with thoughts of his old crew to be bothered with the Bible. While roaming the projects, Tafari was sure to avoid the normal hangout spots of his crew.

Tafari found himself at the pizza shop, pouring quarters into the slots of the video games. By the time Tafari popped in his last quarter, darkness appeared outside of the pizza shop window. The nightlight of the moon was turned off, making the block unusually dark that night.

Tafari left the pizza shop and didn't stop walking until he reached the church. He leaned against the side of the church, unsure of what led him there. His mind was all over the place. The presence of the church awakened memories that were huddled together in the caves of his brain like vampire bats. And just like those rats with wings at sun down, memories of when Tafari first started hanging out on the corner were scattering aimlessly across his brain. The same flock of memories leached onto any random thought that didn't include his life over the last month and sucked the life out of them until they no longer existed in his mind. Tafari's mental filmstrip replayed the beginnings of when he first met up with Lil'

Headache, Stretch, and Los. Tafari closed his eyes and used his mind's eye to watch the journey unfold.

All of a sudden, something chilled the back of Tafari's neck. A presence was felt. His head snapped up. The first thing Tafari saw was a black gun pointing at the medallion that hung from the chain around his neck. He saw a black fist behind the gun. Above the gun was the familiar, menacing face of Dready. Dready's eyes were similar to the eyes he wore the last time he held a gun to Tafari, but that time they were more intense and darker and more piercing. Like a new version of Dready. Angel was by his side. "I told you we would find him," Angel said, pointing in Tafari's face.

"Ya tink ya could just shoot me and get away wit' it?" Dready growled in his raspy Jamaican accent. Dready snapped his head left and right checking out the surroundings before he continued, "I-an-I neva faget. Me have mind like elephant. Every night in Queens me dream 'bout me blood-clot revenge! And now de time has come!"

Tafari's heart was pounding. He seemed to escape death once before, but would he be able to do it again? "Yo, Dready, just take the chain and let's be out?" Angel urged.

"Chill bredren," Dready grunted, turning to Angel. "I'm de originoo Shatta! Him tink he could dispose of I-an-I wit' one shot?! Neva! Me like Iron Man, flesh of steel! And me pack weapon like Iron Man too. Me have new gun and bullet wit' him name 'pon it."

Dready's eyes focused on the chain that dangled around Tafari's neck. "Le' go me blood-clot chain." If Dready lifted the chain from around Tafari's neck, he knew the rep that he built would come crumbling down around him. Stories of Tafari getting robbed by Dready would flood the streets while everyone slept and would headline the street news in the morning. The idea of becoming street prey again made Tafari shutter in fear, even more so than the idea of getting shot by the gun Dready was holding.

There was no way Tafari could allow Dready to remove the chain from his neck, because he wasn't ready to be a part of the morning street news. Tafari coiled up like a snake and lunged at the gun. It exploded in front of him just like the last time he tried to disarm Dready. But unlike last time, it was Tafari who lost control of his legs and crumbled where he stood. It was as if the pavement came up and slammed into the side of Tafari's face. From the pavement he watched as two pairs of Timberland boots ran away from him down the block.

Tafari felt like he was dying. He was trying to hold on, but his life was literally leaking through his fingers. Both palms were sticky red. A red pool was gathering beneath him, forming weird shapes on the concrete like some kind of beautifully grotesque piece of street art that he was finger painting with his own blood.

The cracked pavement was cold beneath his right cheek. Deep within Tafari's core, a flicker of strength remained lit, just enough of a spark to allow him to drag his right shoulder over and collapse onto his back. Tafari's eyes stared deep into the thick blanket of midnight blue, hovering over him as if it was waiting to tuck him in for good.

Tafari managed to lift his head from the concrete, eyes scrambling for someone, anyone, who could help. The old men who were usually sitting on crates in front of the liquor store on the next block were gone. Only the crates remained.

Even though Tafari couldn't see anyone, he knew he was being watched since he lay in the view of hundreds of eyes, lined up on dozens of chipped, red brick buildings. Most of the eyes were bare. Some were shaded with the traditional blinds. Others were covered by colorful bed sheets with cartoon characters posing in fighting stances.

His eyes were scaling and climbing one building in particular, down street on the next block. All of the eyes on the sixth floor were bare except for one. That one eye was closed by a colorful Power Rangers bed sheet. It was the eye he used every night to watch the world beneath it while he sat on the radiator. Tafari couldn't help but wonder if he had stayed behind that window instead of venturing out from behind it and living the life of a street thug, would he be up there looking down on another unfortunate thug who lay on his back bleeding. His eyes dipped below his window and flashed across Mrs. Prier's. It was as if someone snatched her photo from the frame of her window. For the first time in memory, nosy Mrs. Prier didn't have her face in her window. Tafari wondered if she saw him get shot and shut her curtains and did what most people in the projects do: act like she never saw anything.

The faint sound of a siren was heard off in the distance. A jolt of relief surged through Tafari like adrenaline and energized his heavy shell of a body. Usually the sound of a siren is the last thing anyone in the projects wanted to hear. But that night, as he laid helpless on the curb with his life liquids spilling out of him, the sirens were more than a welcomed sound.

As sudden as the sirens appeared, they faded away until they were no longer a part of the projects' noise. Tafari couldn't help but wonder: were the sirens fading, or was he fading? The concrete thumped beneath his cheek and echoed in his ear.

"Tafari, hold on! The ambulance is coming!" a voice yelled. That was the last thing Tafari heard before fading to black.

Chapter 17

Mr. Sekou was the first face Tafari saw when he opened his eyes in the hospital bed.

"Glad to have you back, Tafari," Mr. Sekou greeted through a grin. "You had us worried." Tafari forced a smile while scanning his new surroundings. Tafari's mom raced over and scooped up Tafari in her arms. "Arghhh," Tafari grunted, as pain knifed up his arm and stabbed into his shoulder.

"Oh my God, I'm so sorry, baby," Tafari's mom apologized. "I'm just so overjoyed and blessed to see you open your eyes."

"He's gonna be alright," Mr. Sekou assured. "Luckily he only got hit in the shoulder." Tafari turned his head and analyzed the oversized white bandages covering his left shoulder. He grimaced more from the memory of what happened rather than the aching pain he was experiencing. "How did I get here?" Tafari wondered. "The last thing I remember is lying on the sidewalk and watching my own blood spill into the street. The next thing I know everything goes black."

"Stretch is the reason why you are here," Mr. Sekou revealed.

"Stretch?"

"Yes, Stretch. He said he saw you get shot and he called an ambulance immediately."

"When did he tell you all of this?"

"Earlier."

"He was here? In the hospital?"

"Yes, he was here but you were asleep. He called me as soon as they put you in the ambulance and I met him here."

"Why did he leave?"

"He had to get home but he said he will return tomorrow to check on you."

"I wish he was still here when I arrived," Mom said. "I would have driven him right down to the police station so he could tell them who shot my baby. Did he say anything to you, Mr. Sekou?"

"No. I asked him if he saw the shooter's face but he didn't tell me."

"Did you get a look at him, Tafari?" Mom asked.

"N-no, I didn't," Tafari stammered. Mr. Sekou gave Tafari a look as if he didn't believe him.

"I just can't believe my son is in a hospital bed from a gunshot wound," Mom cut in. "I always thought that if I sheltered my son from the streets, and got him involved in church, which would give him the structure and the morals he needs, that this wouldn't happen."

"Ms. King, the streets don't discriminate," Mr. Sekou said. "It doesn't matter if the teen is church goin', very well educated, or is in a broken home with absentee parents. It's hard for a teen to resist the allure of the streets. Especially when you got your peers pressuring you as well. But if the teen has that structure to fall back on or a vision and a creative imagination, eventually he will find his way out."

"I wanna thank you, Mr. Sekou," Ms. King said, taking Mr. Sekou's hand into hers. "Thank you for caring about my son. Thank you for going above and beyond. We need more teachers like you."

"Thank you for the kind words, Ms. King." Mom dabbed moisture from her eyes and excused herself to the restroom. As she exited, Myles, Big Snacks, and Sha'King entered the room. "Look who's alive!" Big Snacks bellowed. Tafari forced out a smile, as one by one, the boys came over and gave him some dap. "I made you some of my special mac and cheese," Big Snacks announced, setting a small aluminum pan on the food tray beside Tafari's bed. "I put four different cheeses in it."

"Good lookin' out, Big Snacks," Tafari thanked.

"I been cookin' up a storm ever since that discussion we had in Mr. Sekou's class. I think I found my calling."

"Good for you, Big Snacks," Mr. Sekou said.

"Can't wait to try it," Tafari said.

"So how do you feel?" Sha'King asked.

"My shoulder still hurts but other than that I'm good," Tafari said. "I just can't believe I actually got shot."

"Gettin' shot is actually a good thing," Myles said. "It can be good publicity for your rap career."

"Fareal. The only rappers that get better promotion than the ones who get shot are dead ones," Big Snacks joked.

"I think I'll settle for shot-rapper promotion, thank you," Tafari snickered. Everyone laughed.

"I'm glad Tafari is alright and we can joke about it now, but someone needs to do something about all the violence that's been goin' on in the projects lately," Sha'King demanded. "It seems like every other night, someone's been getting shot or jumped. Gangs are poppin' up all over the place too. They need to do something about this."

"Who is they?" Mr. Sekou asked.

"They? The government, right?" Myles asked.

"Do you really think the government is going to come to the projects and try to fix our problems?"

"If they were ever gonna do it, it should be now," Sha'King said. "I mean, we got a black president now. If any president should know what's going on in the ghetto, it would be him."

"I don't disagree with you, but he's America's president and he has to do what's right for all Americans, not just cater to black people," Mr. Sekou reasoned.

"Come on, Mr. Sekou, man," Big Snacks said. "We're not in the classroom. You ain't gotta be politically correct right now. We got a black president right now and it seems like he forgot about us in the hood. Come on, Mr. Sekou, tell us how you really feel."

Mr. Sekou rumbled with laughter. "In all seriousness, you can't sit back relying on someone, or *them*, to save you. Like Gandhi said, 'Be the change you want to see in the world.' If you want something done or changed, you do it. Stop talking about it and be about it."

"You know what, you're right, Mr. Sekou," Sha'King agreed. "I'm gonna be a lawyer, and I'm gonna come back and clean the streets in my neighborhood of all the guns and gangs."

"There you go, Sha'King. Be proactive," Mr. Sekou cheered. A brown-skinned nurse in all white entered the room and said that visiting hours were over. Big Snacks, Myles, and Sha'King gave Tafari dap before exiting the room. Mr. Sekou approached Tafari's bed. "I guess you made your choice, huh?"

"Whatchu mean?"

"You chose your rep over your life?"

"What makes you say that?"

"That bullet wound makes me say that," Mr. Sekou said, pointing at the big white bandage on Tafari's shoulder. "If you would have just given up the chain, there's a good chance you wouldn't have gotten shot." Tafari nodded and rubbed his shoulder. "Luckily, you got a second chance," Mr. Sekou continued. "Not everyone does. My two friends that I told you about earlier, Big Rob and Tone, didn't get a second chance. Just like you, they both had guns pointed at them. And just like you, they didn't want to give up their jewelry because they had reputations. And now, they and their reps are lying in twin pine boxes. Tafari, take advantage of your second chance."

"Thanks for everything, Mr. Sekou." Mr. Sekou shook Tafari's hand and walked to the door.

"One last thing," Mr. Sekou said, standing at the door, smiling. "Just because you got shot doesn't excuse you from writing that essay that you owe me. As soon as you heal up, I expect that essay on my desk." Laughter followed Mr. Sekou as he ducked out of the door. Tafari's mom re-entered the room, briefly, to give Tafari a big hug and promise to return early in the morning with his favorite apple cinnamon pancakes from IHOP.

With the room empty of eyes, Tafari lifted the bottom half of the bandage from his shoulder and let his curious eyes wash over what they've been dying to look at since he opened them. Tafari grimaced at the thick, black stitches that ran up his shoulder. He sealed the bandage back over the wound, and placed his hand on his naked neck. Tafari gazed down to confirm what his hand already knew. His chain was gone. Suddenly, the two choices that Mr. Sekou presented to him danced across his mind: dying for his reputation or living for his future. Tafari looked at the bandage one last time and, suddenly, the choice became obvious.

Tafari King
Mr. Sekou
English 1

Dear Mr. Sekou,

Imagine living in a place where, every night before bed, gun-shots pop like firecrackers on the other side of your window. Imagine living in a place where ambulance sirens are heard more than the laughter of children. Imagine living in a place where stray bullets shatter the dreams of innocent bystanding teens. Imagine living in a place where the adults are so afraid of the gangs that hang on the corner, they lock themselves behind the iron doors of their apartments, scared to walk the streets at night. This place is a jungle; it's a warzone; and it's my home. Despite the many efforts of the police and social activists to eliminate gangs, teens will continue to join gangs because of peer pressure, the lack of a family structure, and the glorifica-tion of gangsters by the media.

First and foremost, as long as peer pressure exists, teens will continue to join gangs. Just take a walk through the concrete jungle known as my neighborhood to witness examples of teens being pressured by their peers to join gangs. Stop by the deli on the corner and watch as a gang of mad-face thugs harass every teenage boy that dares to walk by their turf. Innocent boys who were just passing by on their way home from school are slammed against the brick walls of store fronts and are stripped of all their shiny jewelry and expensive electronics. If they resist, the fists of the gang members will fire into the faces of the teens and the dirty soles of their boots will stomp down on the backs, ribs, and legs of their victims. Eventually, these teens will join the very gangs that were harassing them just to save their pitiful lives because they are tired of getting jumped and robbed. Ninety percent of the teenage boys in my neighborhood are harassed by gangs every day and are forced to make life-changing decisions on a daily basis. Can you really blame the terrified teens for joining the gangs for protection? Seriously, who wants to get jumped and robbed every day of their teenage life? Clearly, many teenage boys are joining gangs because of the stress and anxiety being placed on them by other teens.

Another reason why teens are joining gangs is because they lack a proper family structure. For instance, take a look inside the homes of the gang members, and you'll find that 9 out of 10 live in single-parent homes. I recently read in an article that most teens that join gangs are in underprivileged neighborhoods. Since the single parent is the main bread winner, they usually have to work long hours and sometimes they have to take two jobs just to make ends meet. When this happens, the teen is at home, left to fend for themselves for many hours. This type of teen is vulnerable and is the perfect prey for the savage gangsters to sink their scheming claws into. The gang can offer the teen something he doesn't have: a family. Little does he know, unlike his mother, these so-called brothers will not be there for him for his entire life. They will turn their backs on him the moment the cops slap the cuffs on their wrists. As you can see, living in a broken home can cause teens to turn to gangs.

Pursuing this further, how can a young, influential teen not want to join a gang when the media glorifies the lives of gangsters? I remember when I was 8 years old and I saw my first rap video. I had just gotten home from church and I turned the television on to the video channel. My young eyes watched a group of rappers dressed like gangbangers perform a drive-by shooting and then drive to their mansion to party afterwards. They tossed wads of hundred dollar bills into the air like confetti while the most beautiful girls I ever saw wearing string bikinis clung to the gangster rappers like Velcro. Not only did that rap video teach me that gangsters get all the beautiful women, stacks of money, and fast cars, but it also taught me how to be violent. In addition, it's not just rap videos that glorify gangsters, but also video games. Just like rap videos, these video games glorify guns, drugs, sex, and violence. With the violent rap lyrics in the youths' ears and violent video game images in their eyes, our senses are overloaded with violence. And don't get me started on movies. Obviously, the media plays a huge role in glorifying gangsters.

In the end, as long as teens feel the need to fit in, lack the guidance provided by a structured family, and continue to be influenced by every movie, rap video, and video game they play, teens will continue to be a part of the vicious cycle of gang violence.

Sincerely,

Tafari King

CPSIA information can be obtained
at www.ICGtesting.com
Printed in the USA
LVOW12s1705210716
497247LV00001B/50/P